Tribute

LISA HENRY

CONTENTS

Chapter One: Caralis

"There is no price too high to safeguard the crown."

The philosopher Reiner used to proclaim it vigorously, each word punctuated with the stinging rap of a cane over Kynon's knuckles.

"Pay attention, boy! You'll need to know this one day if, gods forbid, you're ever king!"

Kynon, having a decent grasp on arithmetic and two older brothers who were the pictures of health, had always rolled his eyes at that.

"Well, you'll need to know it anyway," Reiner would say, flicking him on the ear.

No price too high. Kynon had held on to those words for days now and tried desperately to believe them. *"There is no price too high to safeguard the crown."*

To be the son of a king in a time of peace and prosperity was a good thing, and Kynon had known the benefits. To be the son of a king in a time of defeat and hardship was to be a hostage to the Fates. Now, staring death in the face, Kynon understood the costs.

For the last two days Kynon had been confined to the tower with his surviving family. There, in the darkness, he had felt as if he could hardly remember the times of peace and prosperity. The war had lasted for three years, but the shadow of it had been with him for longer. The warlord Brasius was unstoppable. Kingdoms fell before him. In a little over two decades he had conquered half the world for the senate of Segasa. He had the blood of hundreds of thousands on his hands. Caralis was just his latest prize — a small and formerly prosperous kingdom that could not withstand the warlord's armies. Three years ago Brasius had crossed the border. Two nights ago he had taken the capital.

A strange silence had fallen on the castle in the two days since. The servants, if any of them remained, were either forbidden to enter the tower, or too afraid. Kynon had expected to hear the sounds of Brasius's men celebrating and sacking the town, but there had been nothing.

There were almost twenty of them locked in the tower room: Kynon, his brothers, Nemic and Tolan, their mother, two aunts, some cousins, and members of the king's council. There were other rooms in the tower, and Kynon suspected they were all filled with the king's loyal friends and retainers. The queen, Kynon's mother, had wept every night. For the king, Kynon supposed. They hadn't seen the king since the warlord's soldiers had taken the castle. They didn't know if he was even still alive.

And Kynon was afraid. Sitting in the darkness, he wished that he was still young enough to put his head in his mother's lap while she stroked his hair, like a frightened child. He wanted to cling to her and listen to her tell him that it would be all right. Nineteen years old, a prince and a soldier, and he felt like he had when he was five and scared of thunderstorms.

The warlord was like that—a force of nature.

Kynon held his mother's hand at night when she cried, and closed his eyes and tried to recall the words of the lullabies she had once sung to send him safely to sleep.

On the morning of the third day, having spent another uncomfortable and hungry night, Kynon was torn from sleep by the stamping of boots in the passageway outside the tower room and the sound of someone screaming.

"It's my daughter!" Chancellor Varne gasped. "It's Alysia!" He was on his feet instantly. "Alysia!"

Alysia! Kynon thought, jolting upright. He had not seen her since before the final battle. He had not thought of her for longer. She belonged to memory, as if he were an old man instead of a youth of nineteen. She belonged before the war, when she was pretty and sweet and had once refused to kiss him when Conal had dared him to ask.

"I'm going to fight the warlord," he had told her. *"Just one kiss!"*

Blushing, she had fled.

Kynon had seen her once or twice since then, when the warlord's armies had made their winter quarters within the borders of Caralis and the king's army had been given some respite from the war, but those homecomings had been short and Kynon had changed since the coming of the warlord. He had been consumed with strategies then, with seeking out desperate alliances with neighboring kingdoms and countries, with keeping the wolf at bay. Dalliances and love affairs had had no place in his thoughts.

He regretted it now that he was going to die.

"Get back from the door!" someone outside shouted.

Chancellor Varne was not a young or heavy man, but Tolan struggled to pull him back and hold him there as the door swung open and soldiers entered the room.

Light burned Kynon's eyes, and he raised his hand to shield his face.

Over the past few days, they had received several visitations from the warlord's representatives. Priests, Kynon had guessed, both male and female. They wore royal blue robes with an insignia on them that Kynon did not recognize. They had walked among the prisoners slowly, holding their lanterns aloft, looking at faces, asking names, and making notes.

"What do you want?" Tolan had snapped when they asked his name for the third time in a

day. *"What are you doing?"*

The robed man had not answered. He had only made some notation on the paper he carried.

"Tolan! Tolan, don't!" the queen had begged her oldest son. *"Don't! You mustn't!"*

And Kynon had realized in that moment that the robed priests and priestesses were compiling a list of those who would die. The warlord had to first make a show of strength by executing a prescribed number of prisoners, of course, so that later he might look merciful by sparing a few. The thought chilled him, but the next time one of the priestesses pushed her lantern toward his face, Kynon had looked back at her to show her he wasn't afraid.

And when he heard Alysia scream, he knew the appointed hour had come.

This time when the door swung open, it was soldiers only.

"Get back! All of you, down on the floor!" their captain shouted. "Settle down!"

Outside, Alysia's screams turned to sobs, and Kynon's stomach twisted.

The captain consulted a list. "Kynon, son of Jaran, make yourself known."

"No," his mother whispered fiercely. "No!"

Kynon felt Nemic's hand on his sleeve. He shook it off and stood slowly. "I am Kynon, son of Jaran."

"Come with us," the captain said.

Kynon heard a buzzing in his ears. He reached back down to his mother and gripped her hand briefly. "Good-bye."

He heard her sharp intake of breath as the soldiers led him from the room.

*****

Kynon's knees hurt. He was hungry and filthy, but it didn't matter. Kneeling in the throne room with the others, Kynon couldn't shake off his old tutor's words: *There is no price too high to safeguard the crown.*

And now it seemed, against all the odds, it was Kynon who had to pay.

No price too high.

It was true. It was right. It gave him courage because he knew that the alternative was worse. To die or to live in subjugation? It was one of those philosophical questions that got asked late at night before battle. Kynon had always been sure of the answer before. He had fought for freedom, been willing to die for it, but he had lost, and he had lived. That was the worst thing. It would have been easier to die. Dying took but a moment. Living, he knew, was worse. At least he wouldn't have to see Caralis ruled from Segasa. At least he wouldn't have to live with the shame of defeat for long.

It was a terrible thing to think, but even though his mother hadn't wanted him to go, one day she would probably envy him his early death.

A dozen of them were assembled before the warlord Brasius and King Jaran. Jaran looked like he had aged decades since Kynon had last seen him two days before. His father had always seemed proud and strong. Now he looked like an old man. When the soldiers had brought Kynon into the throne room, he had wanted to run forward and embrace his father and had restrained himself with difficulty. They were flies in a web, all of them, and they could not afford to make a misstep.

Kynon found himself kneeling next to Alysia Varne. She was pale and shaking. Kynon thought again of the time he had asked her for a kiss behind the armory wall, three long years ago. He had been sixteen, and she had been fifteen and the loveliest girl he had ever seen. She had golden hair that was the envy of half the town and skin as flawless as alabaster. His friend Conal, seeing the direction of his glances, had teased him about it, goaded him about it, and finally dared him to approach her.

Strange that he hadn't thought of her in so long and today she was all he could think of. It was because he was going to die, he realized. Because he was going to die and he still wished she'd kissed him all those years ago.

Today Alysia hadn't looked at Kynon. She seemed almost insensible, and Kynon doubted she even knew he was there. He wished he could offer her a word of comfort, except he didn't know what to say. He didn't understand what was happening. He looked around the room again.

Kynon saw that all those chosen for execution were young. Some of them had fought against the warlord, but not all of them. And the girls were blameless. They were strange choices for execution. It was their fathers who had wielded influence in the court. Even Kynon, a prince, had older brothers whose executions would be more politically damaging to the crown than his own.

He looked to his father, but Jaran would not meet his gaze.

"Is this them?" the warlord asked, looking at the group.

"Yes, sir," said the captain who had retrieved Kynon. "Selected by your procurators."

"The flowers of Caralian youth!" the warlord said with a skeptical lift of his brows, and the captain laughed.

Kynon risked a look at the man who was going to kill him. Brasius did not look as terrible as his reputation. He was only in his early forties, impressive for a man who had conquered half the world. The warlord was clean-shaven, lean and muscular. His dark eyes were clever and sharp. He wore simple, utilitarian clothes when he could have dressed like an emperor. That was what he was, everyone said, even though he ostensibly served the senate of Segasa. The Segasan senators had a wolf on a leash, Reiner had scoffed, and it would turn on them one day. Not today, though, Kynon thought regretfully. Not in time to save Caralis.

Kynon knew his face.

He had met the warlord once, years ago. It had been in the duchy of Hailon, for the old duke's birthday. Kynon and his mother had attended as the official representatives of Caralis. There had been dignitaries from more countries, kingdoms, and principalities than Kynon could count. He'd been no older than thirteen or fourteen at the time and thrilled by the rumor that the fearsome warlord Brasius would be attending.

Bored with pageantry, Kynon had fallen in with a group of boys around his age. After a few days of awkward overtures, they were all fast friends, politics forgotten. The birthday celebrations didn't interest any of them, and they were very soon the scourge of Hailon Castle. One night, the evening before the old duke's birthday, they had been rushing down one of the narrow corridors in the keep. Kynon, at the head of the pack, hadn't even heard the men before he'd rounded the corner and run straight into them. He'd hit one of them, and the force of the impact had knocked him backward onto the floor. Kynon had landed there, gasping, staring up at the man.

He was a tall man, and broad. His skin was tanned like a commoner's. He had dark hair, an unshaven face, and eyes that looked black in the gloom. He had been dressed no better than a servant, but Kynon hadn't been naive enough to mistake him for one, not even at that age. The man had had the imposing look and bearing of a nobleman.

"*On your feet, boy,*" the man had said, and Kynon, intimidated by the sheer force of authority the man exuded, hadn't even hesitated. He had climbed to his feet, still trying to catch his breath.

The man had looked him up and down like he was waiting for something.

"Servants shouldn't use this passage!" one of Kynon's new friends had exclaimed.

Someone else had hushed him urgently, and in that instant Kynon had known exactly who the man was. The warlord's dark eyes had flashed with something that might have been amusement as the realization had dawned in Kynon. He had stood, his arms folded over his chest, still waiting.

Kynon's heart had thumped. His first instinct had been to apologize, to beg forgiveness, but he hadn't wanted to lose face in front of his new friends. He had drawn himself up and looked up into the man's face. He had folded his arms over his chest, mimicking the warlord's pose, then tilted his chin up and said arrogantly, *"You're in my way!"*

The warlord had narrowed his eyes, and for a moment Kynon had thought he'd strike him. He had felt his heart in his throat.

"Watch your step," the warlord had said at last and passed him.

Kynon's friends had surrounded him, all talking excitedly, confirming what he already knew: *"That was him! That was the warlord, Brasius!"*

Kynon had peered down the hallway, following the warlord with his eyes. As he had watched, the warlord had turned to one of the men with him, and over Kynon's friends' babbling excitement, he had heard the warlord say, *"Find out his name."*

It had terrified him. For months he had been afraid of retribution. He'd had nightmares. Years later when Brasius had set his sights on Caralis, Kynon had wondered if the warlord remembered the boy who had crashed into him in Hailon and refused to apologize. Now, kneeling like a servant in his father's throne room, Kynon felt as though his childhood fears had been realized. The warlord had come for revenge.

His stomach was in knots. He drew a deep, slow breath, trying to calm his nerves while his fate was decided. He could feel the blood pumping behind his ears. Strange, he thought, that even when his mind was resigned to death, his body wasn't: his heartbeat was wild, the hairs on the back of his neck stood up, and he fought the sudden primal urge to run. His body wanted to live.

"Well then, Jaran," said the warlord. "Sign and be done with it."

"My son…" Jaran managed, and his voice cracked.

Brasius narrowed his eyes. "Is one son worth your kingdom, Jaran? I've left you two. This is what you have agreed."

"I didn't know my son would be on the list," Jaran said.

"Tear it up, then," said Brasius. "Tear it up, and I'll install one of my lieutenants in your place and no longer guarantee the safety of your people.

Your choice."

Sign, Kynon willed his father silently. I'll meet my death with dignity.

King Jaran ran a shaking hand through his hair and turned to face the kneeling prisoners. "You are all my subjects," he said. "You are all dear to me. If there are any of you who would not do anything I command, now is the time to speak."

Kynon looked up at his father and couldn't read the king's eyes. Around him, he could feel the others shifting restlessly. Did the king want him to refuse? Did his father really mean to defy the warlord and allow them to escape execution? It was a bold speech, but Kynon found that it only strengthened his resolve. If he didn't agree to this, what then? Would the warlord choose his brothers or, gods forbid, his mother? He didn't want to die. Every sinew in his body screamed it. But to safeguard the crown of Caralis, no price was too high.

None of them spoke.

"Their loyalty does you credit, Jaran," said the warlord.

"Your silence is your consent," the king said, his voice catching in his throat. "May the gods witness it."

Kynon watched as his father signed the document.

"Congratulations, Jaran," Brasius said. "You retain your throne as a client king of the senate of Segasa. I will install several of my advisers on your council, and you will, of course, listen to their experience. You are a free man again and a king."

Jaran gestured at the captives kneeling on the floor. "And them?"

"They will live as long as you remain obedient," said the warlord.

Hostages! Kynon felt a rush of relief and almost sagged to the floor. His eyes widened. They were not to be executed. They were to be the warlord's hostages. He wondered if he could dare to hope they would be treated humanely.

Brasius rose from his seat and came to stand in front of the captives. He studied their bowed heads for a moment and nudged Alysia's knee with his boot. "You. Look at me."

She looked up.

"Is this the prettiest, Captain?"

The captain nodded. "In my opinion, sir, yes."

"Yes," Brasius said. Alysia dropped her head again. "She has some potential. And which one is the prince?"

"Beside her there, sir."

"Show me your face," the warlord commanded, and Kynon looked up. He wondered if the warlord would remember him, but he saw no hint of recognition in the warlord's face. Brasius cast his gaze over him. His eyes lingered on Kynon's mouth. "Very nice."

Kynon jolted in fear at the man's tone.

"It's been some time since we took tributes,"

said Brasius. "Yes, you'll clean up nicely. Captain, divide the other tributes accordingly. Have these two prepared for my own use."

Use? Kynon blanched. The captain pulled him to his feet and forced him from the room. "Father? Father?" he called out, twisting in the captain's grasp. He saw his father standing by his throne, unable to meet his eyes.

*****

The stable yard was a flurry of activity. Tubs of water lined the open space between the stables and the smithy. Segasan soldiers were fetching buckets from the well; water sloshed as they walked, turning the dirt to mud. They were talking, laughing, *joking* like they owned the place. And they did, Kynon realized dully.

The yard was full of the strange priests and priestesses who had inspected the prisoners, all of them wearing the blue robes with the unfamiliar insignia. They watched the approaching prisoners keenly.

Some of the others were crying and struggling, but not Kynon. He couldn't register anything beyond the buzzing in his ears. He couldn't understand what had happened, or he understood only too well. He wasn't sure which. He knew what he had heard, he understood the implications, but he couldn't make himself believe it. It was impossible.

Impossible. He clung to the word as a pair of soldiers manhandled him toward one of the tubs. They stripped him of his soiled clothing and hauled him into the tub. One of the men took a worn scrubbing brush, the sort used on the horses, and began to work it over his flesh.

Kynon looked at the sky. *Impossible.* Except his body didn't believe him anymore. He started to shake. He was standing in a tub, naked, in full view of dozens of people. He should have felt indignant or humiliated, but he was too afraid for that.

He shivered as he recalled the way the warlord's eyes had lingered on his mouth. *"Very nice."* Kynon had never thought of himself as especially good-looking. He was a stripling compared to his brothers. They'd teased him about it since his adolescence. He favored his mother more than his father, with his soft dark hair, his green eyes, and his full lips. He had long dark lashes Tolan had said were girlish. They were only just balanced out by his strong jawline. He had never thought of himself as particularly attractive, but looking around the stable yard, he saw that the others were. The warlord's strange priests must have seen something in him, something Kynon desperately wished he didn't have.

One of the soldiers pulled Kynon from the tub and began to dry him briskly with a rough towel. He felt like a child, standing with his eyes closed and his face screwed up while someone vigorously jiggled his head to dry his hair. The man pulled the towel from his face at last, and one of the blue-robed priests held out a robe for him. Kynon dived into it.

He looked around behind him and saw the other prisoners were being washed and robed as well. He caught a glimpse of Alysia stepping out of the tub, her arms crossed over her breasts, before a soldier swaddled her in a towel. Another stood waiting with a robe.

"Highness!" One of the others caught his wrist. It was Breana, the daughter of the lord of the treasury. Her lovely face was streaked with tears. "We looked to you!"

Kynon felt a stab of guilt. She meant in the throne room. She meant when the king had given them the opportunity to refuse and Kynon had thought it was death they were facing. Would Breana have been so distraught, he wondered, if they were climbing a gallows instead? It was courage again. Kynon had felt he had enough courage to walk bravely to death, just enough to carry him to the end with his dignity intact, but this was something worse.

"I'm sorry," he said. "I'm sorry."

A blue-robed woman clicked her tongue at Breana and pulled her away.

He caught Arron's eye as he was scrubbed down.

Arron—the eldest son of the king's steward. They had stood together on the hills below the town a few days ago, watching the warlord's army approach. The last line of resistance, prepared to face anything. Then they had seen the siege engines and the artillery and had watched in dismay as many of their men had broken and run. The warlord had taken Caralis too easily in the end. Too easily, when they had been ready to die for the crown.

Arron's eyes reflected Kynon's confusion. This was not what they had expected. This was impossible.

The blue-robed priests divided the prisoners, and Kynon found himself beside Alysia again.

"Follow me," said one of the soldiers. Kynon twisted his head to look back at the others, but a second soldier following behind blocked his view and muttered at him to hurry. Then they were back inside the cool darkness of the keep. Kynon almost stumbled on the stairs, and Alysia reached out a hand to steady him. He'd walked these stairs a thousand times before. He could do it in the middle of the night, blindfolded, and today he stumbled. His fear was paralyzing him.

Kynon had never known the castle so quiet. He didn't see another soul as they were led upstairs. The familiar corridors had never seemed more alien. He let his fingers snag against the stone as they walked, just to test if it was real.

The soldiers took them to Kynon's bedroom and locked the door behind them.

Alysia sat beside the bed, her face in her hands. Kynon found himself drawn to the window.

He had stared at the view since the time he was a boy: out over the town, his eyes following the progress of the river as it wound toward the sea. The fertile farmlands on the plains outside the city sometimes looked like a patchwork quilt. Today the plains bristled with the tents and encampments of the warlord's armies.

The room had been cleaned out sometime in the past few days. All his possessions had been removed. Kynon wondered if that was because he was now a hostage or if every room in the castle had been similarly stripped. He hoped it was an accident that he'd been given his own room. Otherwise, it seemed too cruel.

"It's not right," he said to the view. "It's not right."

"Our silence was our consent," Alysia whispered.

Kynon was overcome with a rush of pity and crossed the floor to crouch by her side. "Are you all right?"

"I don't know," she said, her wide blue eyes curiously dull. "I didn't think it would happen like this. I always thought… I always thought…"

"Thought what?" Kynon asked.

"That it would be *you*," she said and ducked her head again.

Kynon flushed.

They both looked up sharply as the door opened and a woman entered. She was wearing a blue robe. It carried the same insignia worn by the people who had chosen them in the tower room and those who had overseen their scrubbing-down at the soldiers' hands.

Kynon regarded her carefully as he rose to his feet.

The woman was not much older than they were. She was lean, with pale skin and dark eyes. She had the proud profile of an aristocrat. Her chestnut hair was pulled back in a braid that went halfway down her back. She radiated authority despite her youth.

"My name is Mistress Hera," she said. "I am chief procurator for the senate of Segasa. You are to be tributes of the warlord Brasius. He has entrusted you to my care." Her cold face softened. "You must be very afraid. I am here to tell you what the senate expects of a tribute."

"I don't know that term," said Kynon.

"You will address me as Mistress Hera," she said.

Kynon flushed and forced his pride down. He had no wish to make an enemy of the woman when she had shown him the first kindness of any of the warlord's people. "Mistress Hera, I don't know what a tribute is."

She smiled at him, seeming pleased by his obedience. "You are a tribute, Kynon. You and Alysia. You are hostages to safeguard your people and your kingdom, but you are also spoils of war. Ultimately you will be displayed as such at a parade in Segasa, after which, if it pleases the senate, you will be allowed to reside in the citadel with some degree of freedom."

"Freedom?" Kynon asked suspiciously. He saw the look on her face, and added, "Mistress."

"Yes," she said. "Many former tributes live in the citadel. Some have been trained at the university. Some have families of their own. Some even serve the warlord on his council."

Traitors to their own people, Kynon thought resentfully.

Hera smiled again as she read the look on his face. "You will find, Kynon, that the warlord is a fair man if you serve him well. To that end, he will fuck you as he pleases, share you with whom he pleases, and you will submit."

Kynon's face burned. Horror and disbelief gripped him as his worst fears were spelled out plainly at last. His father could not have meant for this!

"I see that you have been cleaned," Hera said. "Perhaps not as scrupulously as I would have preferred, but I should not have expected any decent facilities in this backwater."

Kynon bristled. *"Backwater?"*

Suddenly Hera was standing in front of him. He hardly saw her move before he felt the sting of her palm across his cheek. "You will address me correctly!" Kynon was too shocked to react, and Hera smiled again. "And you may change your opinion, Kynon, however little it matters, when you have seen Segasa."

Kynon resisted the urge to rub his face.

Hera leaned in toward him, and he smelled her perfume. "Unless the warlord prefers you masked, in which case you may never see a thing again." She smiled when his eyes widened in horror. "Now let us begin."

Kynon's cheek still stung. He could not recall having been slapped since he was a child, and never on the face. No one would have dared strike a prince, no matter the offense.

"Alysia!" Hera said, and the girl looked up unwillingly. "Stand up, beside Kynon."

Kynon couldn't meet Alysia's eye as she shakily obeyed. There was nothing he could say to comfort her. He couldn't even tell her to be brave, when he had never been so scared before in his life.

"Remove your robes," said Hera. "I will not give you a command twice."

Kynon dropped his robe and stared at the floor. The air was cool on his body. His body. He had never considered it much before. It had been honed by battle and was unblemished except for the narrow scar on his hip. He could still recall the pain as the enemy's sword had glanced off him. It was hardly a scratch, Tolan had assured him, but it had bled freely and had hurt like hell. He had never considered his body as anything more than a vehicle for his mind or as a tool for his will. He had never thought of it as a commodity. He had never had anyone appraise it as frankly and dispassionately as Hera was now.

"Yes," said Hera. "You have a handsome face. You are quite well made, and your cock is a good size."

Kynon flushed and covered himself with his hands.

"Do that again," Hera said, "and you will be punished."

It took all Kynon's will to force his hands back by his sides. He wanted to protest that this was a mistake, that his father could not have intended this, but he was too shocked to speak.

Hera turned her attention to Alysia. "Ah, that's always the way in war. The women suffer privations so the men can keep their strength. You are too thin, Alysia."

Kynon glanced at Alysia without intending it. He saw that she was as lovely as he had once imagined her. She was almost as tall as Kynon. Her figure was more boyish than womanly. She had slim legs, a slender waist, and small, firm breasts. Hera was right, Kynon thought. She could use some more flesh on her. He could count her ribs. He looked away quickly, before she saw him looking at her, and realized with horror that his cock was hardening.

"Yes," Hera said. "With the proper attentions, you will make a pretty pair. Oh, Kynon, I see Alysia is pretty enough for you already."

Alysia glanced at Kynon, and her eyes widened in shock.

"I'm sorry," he said, squeezing his eyes shut.

"On that subject," said Hera, "your master will not tolerate either of you bringing yourself to completion. Do you understand?"

"Please," Kynon said, "I need to speak to my father. He—"

"Do not speak unless it is to answer my question," Hera said. "Insolence and disrespect will be punished. I said that you are not to bring yourselves to completion. Do you understand?"

"Yes, mistress," said Kynon miserably.

"Alysia?"

"I don't know what you mean, mistress."

"I mean," said Hera, "that you are not allowed to touch each another or yourselves without permission. The warlord is your master, and he will tell you when you are allowed to come. Do you understand?"

Alysia didn't answer, and Kynon opened his eyes again. He looked at the girl's face, and it was the picture of confusion. "Mistress, she doesn't know what you mean."

He almost envied her that.

Hera looked at Alysia intently. "Are you a virgin, Alysia?"

"Yes," the girl whispered.

"And have you never touched yourself?" Hera asked. She sighed at Alysia's incomprehension and reached out to cup the girl's pubic mound. Alysia recoiled from the woman's touch.

"Oh gods!" Kynon said, shocked, before he could stop himself.

Hera looked at Kynon, eyebrows raised. "You can keep your backward morality to yourself, tribute." She pressed her hand more firmly against Alysia. "Here, Alysia. Your cunt. Have you ever worked your fingers in it and come?"

Alysia squeezed her eyes shut and shook her head. "No!"

Hera withdrew her hand. "Another casualty of war, I expect. All the young men are on the battlefield, neglecting their duties at home. Never mind, Alysia. In a day or two you will be more experienced than most whores."

Alysia's hands flew to her mouth as she cried out.

Kynon tensed with sudden anger and took a step toward Hera.

She didn't even flinch. "I will warn you once, Kynon. Raise a hand to me, and you will regret it."

Kynon believed it and stood back. His face burned.

"While you serve your master, you will be naked," said Hera. "You will be collared and chained, as is the senate's pleasure. When your master enters the room, you will be on your knees. Kneel."

They obeyed.

"Put your hands behind your necks," said Hera. "Spread your knees. That is the position you are to assume in your master's presence and in the presence of your betters until you are commanded otherwise. Any deviation from the position will result in whatever punishment your master sees fit. If you do not submit willingly, you will be whipped into submission. Do you understand?"

"Yes, mistress," said Kynon.

"Yes, mistress," Alysia whispered.

"Good," said Hera. "In Segasa, in a month, you may be required to undergo further refinement. I promise you that your attitudes will have been adjusted by the time we reach the citadel. In the meantime, you will obey me as you would your master. That is all for now."

She scooped up their robes from the floor and took them with her.

After she left, Alysia started to cry.

Chapter Two: Tribute

Kynon leaned against the door. "I want to see my father! I demand to see my father!"

He pounded on the door.

Alysia, sitting curled up at the foot of the bed, didn't try and stop him.

The hours had passed slowly since Mistress Hera had left them, until Kynon, wound as tightly as a spring, hadn't been able to stand it anymore.

The anticipation was the worst, Kynon thought, and he expected he'd go on thinking it until the warlord actually... Well, until it happened. But for now it was the waiting that tormented him—a psychological torture that felt worse than anything the warlord could inflict. Kynon had allowed his anger to build. He had every right to feel outraged. He wasn't just going to sit here like a dumb animal and wait. He wasn't a prize of war. He wasn't a *thing*.

"I demand to see the king!" he shouted at the door. His fists hurt, and blood oozed from his knuckles.

The door swung open suddenly, and Kynon

sprawled backward onto the floor.

The same captain who had overseen their scrub-down in the stable yard stood on the threshold. He looked down at Kynon and didn't smirk at his nakedness or seem embarrassed for him.

"What's all this noise?" he asked.

"I want to see my father!" Kynon said, climbing to his feet.

"He doesn't want to see you," the captain said.

"That's a lie!" Kynon exclaimed, although there was nothing in the man's face to suggest it.

The captain only shrugged. He was not a tall man, but he was broad. Kynon could see the cords of muscle in his forearms. He was in his thirties, tanned, and there was a trace of amusement in his green-gray eyes.

Mistress Hera, when she appeared behind him, had a face like stone. "What is going on here, Rennick?"

The captain nodded his head deferentially. "The tribute was making a fuss, Mistress Procurator."

"Indeed," said Hera, turning her blazing eyes on Kynon. "And he's already forgotten the position!"

Alysia, Kynon saw belatedly, had not. She was kneeling with her knees apart and her hands behind her neck.

Hera sighed. "Take him to the stable yard,

Rennick."

"Yes, Mistress Procurator," said the captain. He was matter-of-fact. He held Kynon still while he tried to struggle, and buckled a leather collar around his neck.

"Don't touch me!" Kynon twisted and squirmed in his grasp, but the captain was too strong for him.

The captain hauled him from the room.

Kynon's bare feet could hardly get purchase as he was dragged along the passageway. He stumbled when he hit the steps, and the captain kept him from falling by pulling back on the collar. Kynon struggled for breath. One of the maids, meeting them on the steps, gasped and dropped the tray she was carrying. It crashed to the stones, and the sound echoed loudly.

"You make a scene, you get an audience," said the captain as other servants came running.

Kynon was humiliated but still struggled to be free.

Rennick dragged him farther down into the keep.

The sunlight, when it hit Kynon in the face, almost blinded him. The captain dragged him across the stable yard and threw him to the ground. Then he took a piece of leather and bound Kynon's wrists tightly together in front of him. As Rennick was bending over him, Kynon tried to get a knee into the man's groin, but Rennick was too quick for him. He pressed Kynon onto the ground with a hand on his throat.

Kynon choked for breath.

Rennick watched him carefully. Just as Kynon thought the man meant to kill him then and there, he released the pressure on Kynon's throat. Kynon gasped, rolling onto his side.

"There now," said Rennick casually. "Behave yourself."

Kynon tasted mud. His head was throbbing, his lungs ached, and he could hear men laughing.

Rennick hauled him to his knees. "Stay."

Kynon looked around and saw that the warlord himself was in the stable yard with several of his generals. Brasius's dark eyes were hooded, and his handsome face gave nothing away. He was leaning against the wall of the keep, watching.

Kynon saw another familiar face: Conal. Conal had been his best friend since childhood, ever since Ambassador Trefus had come to Caralis from Lutrica to take up his diplomatic position and brought his son along with him. What Conal was doing talking with Brasius, the enemy, Kynon had no idea. Perhaps Trefus had sent his son to flatter and admire the warlord, even though it was probably already too late to try to influence the man with courtly pleasantries. Lutrica would be next, now Caralis had fallen. It was as inevitable as the dawn.

Conal's golden hair, flyaway on the breeze, caught the sunlight. His face was pale, and his eyes widened with shock as he caught Kynon's gaze.

Kynon, mortified at having his friend see him like this, didn't even hear the *swish* of the whip through the air before the narrow tails caught him on the back. His whole body lifted off the ground, his back arched, and his breath was knocked out of him. The pain was sudden and intense. It spread across his flesh like fire. He felt like he'd been cut to the bone.

He didn't scream the first time. He didn't have the breath. The second time the whip caught him, aimed squarely between his shoulder blades so that the tails curled up over his shoulders and around his neck, Kynon screamed. He was sure the captain was going to kill him.

Through eyes flooded with tears, he saw Brasius still watching. And Conal as well, frozen to the spot in horror.

Kynon couldn't count the strokes. They bled together. He tasted blood when he bit the inside of his cheek, and tasted mud when he fell forward onto the ground. He didn't know how long he lay there before Rennick threw a bucket of water over him to revive him. It hit his back like burning oil, and he sucked in a mouthful of mud and started to choke.

Kynon saw boots in front of his vision.

"Only five, Rennick?" the warlord asked, and Kynon heard the smile in his voice.

"I must be going soft, sir," Rennick said.

Kynon flinched at the cautious touch of a hand against his shoulder. "Kynon?" It was Conal.

"Are you all right?"

"Stand up, Conal," said the warlord in an amused voice. "The ambassador needs to tell you that it is not appropriate to touch another man's spoils of war."

Rennick hooked his hand through Kynon's collar and pulled him back up to his knees. He swayed there until his eyes found the warlord's face.

"I want to see my father," he managed.

Something like surprise passed across the warlord's face at the audacity, and then it was gone again. He ignored Kynon and turned to Conal instead. "Tell the ambassador I have no time to see him presently."

"Yes, sir," Conal stammered, executing a clumsy bow before he fled the stable yard.

Kynon kept his gaze fixed on the warlord's face. He wanted to scream, to spit, to fight, to do something, but he didn't have the strength. "I want to see my father," he repeated.

The warlord looked at him curiously. "He has spirit, Rennick."

"Yes, sir." Rennick pressed a cup against Kynon's lips. "Drink. It'll take the sting away."

Kynon obeyed. The liquid tasted strange, and almost immediately the pain in his back defused. It throbbed no worse than sunburn now.

Rennick pulled Kynon to his feet and hauled him through the castle again, up the stairs to his old bedroom. When Rennick pushed the door open,

Kynon saw Alysia, her eyes squeezed shut, lying on the bed with her parted legs hanging over the edge.

Kynon, leaning heavily against Rennick, felt the man's cock suddenly harden and jab him in the hip. Despite his discomfort, Kynon wasn't immune to the sight either.

Mistress Hera, standing between Alysia's legs, looked up at them as they entered. She stepped away. "Assume the position."

Alysia scrambled to the floor quickly.

Rennick hauled Kynon over to the end of the bed and attached him by a length of chain to the bottom bedpost. He did the same to Alysia, while Hera inspected the marks on Kynon's back.

Kynon shivered as Hera trailed her fingers over the stinging, swollen ridges of his flesh. He cried out when she suddenly raked her nails down his spine.

"This is nice work, Rennick," she said.

"Thank you, Mistress Procurator."

Rennick gave Kynon more of the strange drink and then offered the cup to Alysia. Then he and Hera left, and the awful day wore on.

Kynon shifted uncomfortably on the floor.

"Are you all right?" Alysia whispered at last.

He hunkered over. "Is there much blood?"

Alysia made sympathetic sounds. "Only a little."

Kynon swore under his breath. "Felt like bucketloads."

"Your Highness," Alysia whispered, "when

do you think it will happen?"

"Don't call me that, please," he said. "I don't know."

Nightfall, he thought. It seemed apt for such indignities to be suffered in darkness, but the sun was still in the sky when they heard the latch opening on the door.

They both climbed to their knees quickly. His hands behind his neck, Kynon looked across at Alysia. He envied her long hair. With her head bowed, her golden hair shielded her face like a curtain. Kynon wished he had something to protect his shame.

Brasius stood before them. "You have learned the basics well. One of you a little slower than the other, of course."

Kynon flushed, and his back burned.

Brasius exhaled. "Were you sent to me as voluntary tributes, I would have allowed you both some time for proper training. However, we must travel to Segasa as soon as possible, and you will both submit before that happens. I will take you by force if I must, but I would prefer your compliance."

Kynon raised his face and dared to look into the warlord's dark eyes. "It is still force, whether we comply or not."

The warlord's mouth curled into a slight smile. "It is a different kind of force and infinitely more preferable for you, for your family, and for this kingdom. I do not tolerate oath-breakers. Do you understand me?"

"Yes." Kynon tried not to flinch away as the warlord reached forward to touch his hair. The warlord ran his hand through his hair and partway down his back, and the slight touch reawakened the pain of his welts. His back throbbed and—to Kynon's horror—so did his cock. He didn't understand his body's reaction to the man's touch and wondered if it had something to do with the strange drink Rennick had given him. Of course it was some sort of drug; it had eased his pain immediately. Apparently that was not its only effect.

"You are quite lovely." The warlord glanced at Alysia. "Both of you."

Kynon stared fixedly at the floor. He wondered which one of them would suffer the warlord's attention first and hated himself for hoping it was Alysia.

To Kynon's surprise, and to his relief, Brasius seemed to lose interest in them. He crossed to the desk that had been Kynon's until two days before and sat there. Moments afterward, the door to the room opened again. Rennick entered with papers in his hands. A soldier followed him with a tray of food, and Kynon's stomach growled. He couldn't remember how long it had been since he'd eaten, and he tried not to let his hunger show on his face.

Rennick set the food on the desk, and Brasius ignored it. Instead, he turned his attention to the papers. With Rennick standing by his side, he began to work through them. Occasionally he spoke in a low voice, and the captain answered, but Kynon could not make out the words.

The muscles in Kynon's shoulders and thighs began to ache. He longed to change his position, but he didn't dare. Instead, he bowed his head, closed his eyes, and wished he'd died on the battlefield. Anything rather than this.

"Rennick, fetch them."

The captain crossed the floor, and Kynon felt the jerk of the chain on his collar as he was unchained.

"Stand," said the captain, removing the chain from Alysia's collar as well. He nodded toward Brasius. "Go and kneel before your master."

Reluctantly, Kynon crossed the floor to the desk with Alysia at his side.

Every muscle in Kynon protested as he knelt again and clasped his hands behind his neck. His knees hurt.

He heard the door open and close again and realized the captain had left. They were alone with the warlord. Kynon chest swelled with hope. Could they overpower the man?

The warlord seemed to read his thoughts. "My army occupies this town. It could be ashes by tomorrow."

Kynon bowed his head.

"Look here," the warlord said. He was holding a piece of parchment before them. "Here are your names. Here is your king's signature. You are the price of peace. Do you understand?"

"Yes, master," Alysia whispered.

Kynon forced the words out from behind his clenched teeth. "Yes, master."

Brasius took a piece of bread into his hands and tore a piece from it. He held it out to Alysia. "Open."

Alysia parted her lips hesitantly, and Brasius pushed the bread inside her mouth. Then he held out a piece to Kynon.

Fed scraps like dogs, Kynon thought mutinously, but after so long in the tower, he was too hungry to refuse. His mouth watered, and his stomach growled again. The touch of Brasius's fingers against his lips made his skin crawl, but he took what he was offered, and hoped for more.

"Are you hungry, my tributes?" Brasius said with a laugh. He held out a cup of wine. "Are you thirsty?"

Kynon felt the cup against his lips and cautiously tilted his head back to drink. It was wine, but there was no mistaking the added taste. It was the same stuff he'd been given after his whipping. Brasius angled the cup quickly, and wine spilled down Kynon's naked chest and dribbled down to his groin. He almost choked, and struggled not to wrench himself away as Brasius forced him to drink.

He gasped for breath as he watched Alysia undergo the same treatment. She could not drink fast enough either; her throat and breasts glistened with wine, and Kynon's cock twitched.

Brasius rose and walked around behind them.

Alysia cried out as the warlord pulled her to her feet and then turned and pushed her onto the desk. He arranged her so that she was lying back with her buttocks and legs hanging over the desk. She clenched her hands into fists and closed her eyes as she began to cry.

The warlord pulled his shirt over his head. His body was lean and muscular and not unscathed by battle. His shoulders were broad, but his torso tapered down to a waist that was narrow. He carried no spare flesh. He was a man who led his armies from the front. He unfastened his belt and let it fall to the floor and then removed his leggings.

Kynon's eyes widened as he saw the warlord's hard cock. It was large, surely too large. It was long and thick, the swollen head dark with blood, and rampant. Brasius took it in one hand, and with the other, he reached forward and opened Alysia.

"Hera says you are a virgin," he said. "Relax your muscles."

From his position on the floor, Kynon couldn't see what the warlord was doing with his hand, but Alysia twisted back and forth on the table. "No, please, no!"

"Did you read your name on the charter?" the warlord demanded. "Did you?"

"Yes," she whispered.

"And will you obey your king by giving me

your consent?"

"Yes." It was no louder than a breath.

Kynon didn't want to watch Alysia's humiliation, but he couldn't make himself look away. He wanted to be sick, and he didn't know if it was too much wine on an empty stomach or something else. Why couldn't he look away?

When he was sixteen, he had fantasized about Alysia, trying to imagine what her naked body looked like underneath her modest dresses. He'd thought of her when he'd visited the whorehouses in the town, imagining the whores he paid were as pretty as her. Imagining it wasn't a transaction. He'd thought of her like this as well, naked in the daylight, her legs apart. Except he'd imagined he was the man standing between them.

And so, he thought with shock, had Alysia.

She hadn't been crying in his fantasies. Ashamed, Kynon still couldn't look away as he saw the tendons in Brasius's arm tighten as he moved his hand between Alysia's legs.

Brasius released his cock and reached for the jug of wine on the table. He held it above Alysia and then tipped it slowly and deliberately over her body. When the liquid hit her flesh, Alysia arched her spine upward in surprise, and her eyes flashed open. They widened as Brasius leaned forward to taste the wine.

Kynon felt his cock throb as Brasius lowered his mouth onto Alysia's small breast. Alysia gasped as the warlord's lips closed around her nipple. She opened her fists into trembling fingers. Brasius tasted one breast and then the other, and all the while his hand was working away somewhere between her thighs.

"Please," Alysia managed, but the sound died away in a murmur.

Kynon saw the moment that she began to respond. She arched her spine again, and she opened her knees wider.

Brasius pushed his cock into her. She whimpered, and he twisted her nipple between his thumb and forefinger. Then he began to thrust.

Kynon couldn't take his eyes off Alysia. Her pale skin, stained with wine, flushed slowly with heat. She lifted herself from the desk, pushing her shoulders back as the warlord again lowered his mouth toward her breast. Kynon saw her gasp, and he realized the warlord had used his teeth on her sensitive flesh. Kynon's cock twitched.

Brasius stood upright. He gripped Alysia's hips and pulled her farther off the desk, impaling her totally on his massive cock. Then he hooked his arms under her knees, and she gasped as he began to thrust more rapidly. She writhed on the desk, her hands fluttering.

"Come for me, girl," the warlord growled, and Alysia arched her back and shuddered. She gripped the edges of the desk tightly as she came and cried out.

Kynon almost came at the ragged sound of it.
Brasius pulled out, his cock red and still

engorged. He was breathing heavily, and his muscular body shone with sweat. He turned his face to Kynon. "Hands and knees, boy, now."

His stomach churning, his heart pounding, Kynon obeyed. This was the price of peace, he told himself. If he did this, nobody else in Caralis had to die.

"Give me your consent," Brasius demanded.

Kynon didn't answer. Fear overwhelmed him. He couldn't do this. He wasn't strong enough to do this. He understood the mechanics, or supposed he did. His experience with women was limited enough. The only things he knew about the sexual act between two men had been gleaned from dirty jokes and snide insults. They weren't funny now. Every instinct told him this would hurt like hell.

"Your consent," Brasius repeated.

Kynon squeezed his eyes shut. "My silence is my consent!"

"Not good enough!"

Kynon steeled himself. There was no price too high to safeguard the crown. Nobody else had to die. He said through clenched teeth, "Yes."

He tensed as liquid, too viscous to be wine, flowed down his lower back and between his buttocks. Oil? It trickled down to his balls and cock. He was terrified.

"Legs farther apart," said Brasius, and then Kynon felt the warlord's finger pressing around his anus, probing him. He felt the muscles yield, and the finger pushed inside him. Kynon's face burned at the indignity of it. He had no time to adjust to the strange sensation before a second finger joined the first. Brasius thrust his fingers in and out, scissoring them, stretching him. The sensation was uncomfortable, his lower back tensed and ached, and then the warlord pulled his fingers away.

Kynon choked back a sob as Brasius dug his fingers into his hips, and he realized the warlord was in position. His resolve vanished.

"Please," he said, suddenly shivering. "Oh gods, please don't."

The warlord's breath was hot against his ear. "This is going to hurt, princeling."

The tip of the warlord's cock pressed against his anus. Kynon panicked. It was too big.

"Please don't!" he said again, feeling the words catch in his throat as the warlord forced his cock inside him.

It hurt more than anything Kynon had experienced. It was excruciating. His cock went limp. Tears burned his eyes. He tried to throw Brasius off, but the warlord was too strong. Brasius gripped his hair and pulled his head back roughly.

"If you fight me, boy, it will hurt even more!"

Kynon began to cry. The pain in his anus, in his back, was awful.

Brasius began to thrust. "Can you feel that? Tell me how it feels!"

Kynon felt as though his flesh was being torn apart. He tried to force himself to relax, to just take it, but he was too afraid and in too much pain. His anus was impossibly stretched. His muscles screamed their protest at the intrusion. He felt as though his spine were being crushed. He just wanted it to be over.

"Tell me how it feels!" Brasius demanded. He pulled his hand down through Kynon's hair and gripped the leather collar around his neck. He tugged on it sharply.

"It hurts!" Kynon wept. His hands and knees scraped across the floor as the warlord thrust.

The warlord growled, "You are so fucking tight!"

Kynon felt the warlord shudder, and then a blast of heat deep inside as he came. Brasius didn't withdraw but only ran a hand up and down Kynon's aching spine, reigniting every welt across his back.

Kynon tried to stop his tears. The pain was less now that Brasius was no longer hard, but he was so utterly humiliated that he couldn't stop crying.

Brasius withdrew. "Lie on your back, boy."

Kynon didn't want the other man to see his face, but he didn't dare disobey. He lay on the floor, the cool stones almost soothing against his burning skin, and shuddered in disgust as warlord's warm semen leaked out of his abused body.

Kynon struggled for breath, wiping away his tears.

Brasius knelt over him and closed his hand

over Kynon's cock. "I could fuck you all day, boy."

Kynon's breath caught in his throat. The feel of the warlord's hand on his cock was astonishing. No one had ever touched him like that. He could feel the calluses in the warlord's palm rubbing against his most sensitive flesh. His cock twitched and began to harden.

The warlord rubbed his thumb over the head of Kynon's cock, spreading the droplet of clear fluid across the throbbing head.

Ashamed, Kynon turned his face away and found himself looking at Alysia. She lay where the warlord had left her on the desk, flushed and naked and despoiled. Her gaze caught Kynon's and held it.

"That's it," said Brasius, following his gaze. "Look at her. One day I might let you fuck her if you please me. Fuck her as hard as you want." He began to stroke Kynon. "As hard as I fucked you."

Kynon forgot the pain in his ass. He groaned as Brasius worked one hand over his cock. His cockhead glistened with precum.

Brasius took Kynon's balls in his other hand, gripping them firmly.

Kynon gasped.

"Look at her," Brasius commanded, stroking him faster. "Look at her, tribute, and come for me!"

Kynon's balls constricted. He shuddered and gasped on the floor as he came over the warlord's hands. The shame of coming into another man's hand was almost worse than having been fucked.

To be fucked was to be a passive victim. To come was different.

Brasius held up his hands, which were covered in strings of Kynon's semen. Slowly, deliberately, he rubbed his hands along Kynon's chest to clean them while Kynon twisted away in disgust.

The warlord rose to his feet and beckoned Kynon to stand. Taking him by the collar, he dragged Kynon back to the end of the bed and fastened the chain to the collar. Kynon stood there, shivering.

Brasius reached out and touched his cheek. The touch was almost gentle. "Tomorrow you will walk through this castle, and everyone will know I've fucked you. You will be ashamed, humiliated, and one day, just the memory of it will make you come."

Kynon shook his head.

The warlord dropped his hand and squeezed Kynon's cock. "I promise you."

Kynon pushed his hips forward and blushed as he saw Brasius smile.

"Rest," said the warlord, releasing him. "Rest while you can."

*****

Collared and chained, Kynon slept at the foot of his old bed. All the muscles in his body ached from the whipping, from kneeling, from submitting to the warlord. His tiredness overcame his wild thoughts, and he slept for several hours. It was night when Kynon was awoken by a sharp tug on his collar. For a moment he didn't remember where he was or what had happened, and the realization he was chained like a dog hit him hard in the stomach. He peered up through the gloom and saw the wide-shouldered figure of the captain looming above him.

"Get up now," the captain whispered, "if you need to piss."

Kynon climbed to his feet. His whole body ached. He looked over to the bed, to *his* bed, and saw the warlord sleeping there. Brasius was lying on his back, one arm outflung. He looked too peaceful for a monster, and Kynon's skin crawled.

Rennick tugged the chain, and Kynon shuffled behind him toward the door.

Once he was out in the hallway, he could hear the sound of music drifting up from the direction of the hall. It surprised him.

"Your father," Rennick said with a knowing smile, "would rather not hear the noises coming from this wing tonight. He has ordered the musicians to play through until dawn, just in case."

"I want to see him," Kynon said. His throat ached with tears.

The captain looked him in the eye. "But he doesn't want to see you, tribute."

And Kynon realized it was true. Tears pricked his eyes.

Rennick's tone was almost kind. "Come on. It's all right."

Rennick led him down the servants' stairs, and Kynon was glad. He would have hated to meet a nobleman or a family member on the main stairs. The captain stood behind him in the garderobe while he pissed. He cleaned his hands in the bowl of water provided, but Rennick pulled him back before he could wash the stains off his chest. Kynon flushed, realizing he smelled like sweat and cum.

In the night stairs, heading back toward his old bedroom, a figure slipped down toward them.

"Kynon? Kynon? Is that you?"

Kynon's heart skipped a beat. "Conal?"

He could hardly make out his friend's face in the gloom as Conal picked his way down the stairs.

"Sir!" Conal said to the captain. "Please, I'll give you half a crown if you let me speak a moment with my friend."

"You can speak all you want," the captain said levelly, "in the time it takes me to return him to his place, but I won't be bought."

He pulled on the chain again, and Kynon fell into step behind him. "What's happening?" he asked.

"I don't know," Conal said. "The warlord, he's, um, he's changing everything. His men are examining the treasury now. He's dissolved the council!"

"What about my family?" Kynon asked, glad the darkness offered him some protection from

Conal's sympathetic gaze.

"They're well," Conal said. His voice cracked. "Are *you*?"

They were in the corridor outside his bedroom now, and Kynon was almost relieved to be back. How could he even begin to answer that question? If he tried to articulate his thoughts, the shame and the horror, he knew he wouldn't be able to maintain his composure. It was difficult enough without acknowledging what had happened. To face it would be wrenching.

"You should go back to Lutrica," he said. "You and your father, and forget about us."

"Kynon!" Conal's anguished whisper came close to breaking him.

"Time's up," said Rennick. He led Kynon back inside the bedroom and shut the door firmly. He attached the chain to the end of the bed again and crouched beside Kynon. In the darkness his face was unreadable, but his voice sounded sincere. "You were almost right, tribute."

Kynon felt a chill.

He heard the smile in the captain's voice and tried not to flinch as the captain gave him a sympathetic pat on the shoulder. "But it's not them who need to forget. It's you."

*****

When Kynon awoke, it was barely light outside, and at first he didn't know what had woken him. Then he realized he could hear the warlord grunting, and he turned his head in the gloom to look. Alysia was kneeling on the floor, chained to the other bedpost, and Brasius was fucking her mouth. Her eyes were closed. Brasius held her head in his hands and thrust into her face. As Kynon watched, he pulled her head toward him roughly.

How was she not choking? Kynon's eyes widened as Brasius withdrew his massive cock from Alysia's mouth and then pushed in again.

Kynon's cock hardened.

"You will swallow it all," Brasius said, and Alysia made some noise that might have been assent. Kynon watched as Brasius's buttocks clenched and his muscular legs tensed. He grunted as he came, and Alysia swallowed furiously.

"Good girl," said Brasius, pulling out and stroking her hair. Alysia opened her eyes. She was panting with exertion. Brasius reached out and pinched her left nipple, and Alysia moaned softly. "You did well, girl. Tomorrow you will do better."

"Yes, master," Alysia whispered and bowed her head.

Brasius turned and saw Kynon watching. He smiled as he took in Kynon's hard cock. "No more tonight, little prince. You must keep your strength. Tomorrow we travel over some rough country."

*****

Brasius had promised humiliation, and

Kynon's face burned the moment the door was opened. He and Alysia were naked, unwashed from the previous night, and their hands were shackled behind their backs. Captain Rennick led them by chains attached to their collars.

"Make way!" he called out as they descended the stairs into the main rooms of the castle. "Make way for the tributes of the warlord Brasius!"

The throne room was full of people. Kynon had resolved to keep his eyes down.

"Kynon! Kynon!" his mother cried out, and the room was suddenly silent.

Kynon looked up at the sound and regretted it at once. His mother was horrified. Her hands flew to her pale face, and she tried to push toward him. The king restrained her. Kynon saw his brothers standing beside their father. Tolan looked aghast, and Nemic's face was set like thunder. Kynon looked at his father.

Now was the time for the king to make his objections known. Now was the time for him to rip up the treaty and cry that he hadn't known what it meant to give his son and the others to the warlord. But he couldn't even meet Kynon's eyes.

Kynon felt a rush of anger toward his father. How could he have agreed to this? How could he have allowed it? Reason told him his freedom and the freedom of the other tributes were a small price to pay to save Caralis, but *this*? He would have preferred to die.

"Alysia!" Chancellor Varne's voice was reed

thin.

Every nobleman and wealthy citizen of Caralis must have been in the throne room that day, desperate to hear from the king how their lives had been spared, what form their subjugation would take, and what price Jaran had paid to the warlord. Every one of them saw Kynon's shame.

Kynon understood then why Brasius had made them submit in Caralis. The people had to see it. The people had to see the warlord's power and, by extension, the might of Segasa. More than that, Jaran had to see it. He had to see his son humiliated and brutalized, and he had to understand that if Brasius willed it, the same thing would happen to Tolan and Nemic and to every nobleborn youth in the kingdom. He had to know there were worse choices than risking his sons in battle.

Kynon caught a glimpse of Ambassador Trefus and Conal. The pale face of the ambassador suggested Trefus had seen the cost of resistance.

Kynon looked away before he caught Conal's gaze.

"Make way!" Rennick called out again. "Make way for the tributes of Lord Brasius!"

The room was full, but Kynon had never known it to be so deathly quiet. He bowed his head and tried not to cry. Beside him Alysia began to weep.

The captain jerked on their chains, causing Alysia to stumble into Kynon. They jostled against each other to try and maintain their balance.

Nobody stepped forward to help them. Kynon heard someone toward the back of the room start to cry: gasping, throaty sounds that reminded him of the noises he had made when he'd come in the warlord's hands.

When they left the throne room and the doors were closed after them, the captain released the tension on the chains.

"Come on now," he said, leading them out toward the private garden courtyard. Kynon had always thought of it as his mother's garden. It had always been her sanctuary. Today it was full of men wearing the livery of the warlord.

Rennick pushed Kynon and Alysia into the hands of a man wearing the same insignia on his robes as Mistress Hera: a procurator. He, in turn, passed them on to a pair of underlings, who began to scrub them down with warm, soapy water.

Kynon looked around at the activity.

The gates to the main stable yard were open, and Kynon could see carts being loaded. There were two large crates near the gates, with more procurators fussing around them.

The warm water soothed his aching muscles a little, and he closed his eyes as a pair of knowing hands began to knead the muscles in his shoulders. The welts on his back stung less this morning.

"Drink this," someone said and pushed a cup into his face.

It was the same herbal concoction the captain had given him the day before to dull his pain, and the same that Brasius had made him drink sweetened with wine. It was pleasant, and Kynon was thirsty and didn't resist as the liquid was tipped into his mouth.

One of the underlings began to rub him down with a towel. Kynon glanced across to Alysia. She looked lovely standing naked in the sunlight with her eyes closed and her face turned up to the sun. Kynon's cock thickened despite himself, and the man toweling him down patted him on the hip.

A second man approached and began to rub scented oil into Kynon's flesh, paying particular attention to the muscles of his abdomen. The man rubbed his hands lower, and Kynon's cock twitched, but the man's attention was perfunctory.

Beside him, Alysia gasped, and Kynon saw another man sliding an oiled hand between her thighs. The man said something in an undertone; the procurator laughed, and Alysia flushed with shame.

Captain Rennick came over to inspect them as they glowed in the sunlight. "All right," he said to the procurator and his men, "let's box them up for transport. Take a good look, tributes. You won't see Caralis again."

Chapter Three: The Journey

When the crate was closed, Kynon was terrified. He was bound, suspended by a web of silk scarves, none of them thin enough to do more than mark his flesh. The silk smelled of something sweet that he couldn't place. It was almost too strong. It was intoxicating and made him drowsy. The combination of the perfume and the liquid he had drunk before being put in the crate went straight to his cock.

Kynon had been unable to see what was being done to him as he was being bound. The captain and the procurator had lowered him into the crate, onto the webbing, and then the captain had tied his hands underneath him. Kynon, breathing in the horsey, earthy smell of the captain, had been unable to see beyond the man. Someone had twisted a plug inside his anus, and Kynon had cried out. It wasn't until the crate had been closed and then shifted that Kynon had realized the plug was attached to the crate. The movement of the crate caused Kynon to rock gently in the soft webbing, moving back and forth on the unyielding plug. The contours of the plug rubbed against a place deep inside him, and his cock hardened in response. Kynon hadn't known that being penetrated could feel good. The night before, consumed with pain and panic, he hadn't allowed himself to feel it. Now, in the anonymity of the darkness, Kynon found himself wondering if he could gain enough leverage to fuck himself on the plug until he came, but the cunning bindings did not allow him enough movement. He lay there instead, held in a constant state of arousal.

He heard the sounds of familiar activity outside: horses and men. The crate was lifted; Kynon groaned as the plug drove into him, and then he heard the creak of cartwheels and he was being transported away from the only home he had ever known, surrounded by the army he had once faced in battle.

He lost track of time. He couldn't tell if he'd been in the crate for an hour or for days. Strange thoughts assaulted him. He thought that maybe he'd slept and maybe he'd dreamed, but he couldn't tell. He was overcome with sensation. He was losing his mind. He cried as well, in moments of awful clarity, because he was being taken away, because he was a slave, and because his entire family had witnessed his humiliation. But sometimes he didn't remember at all. It came in waves. When his body trembled with arousal and he felt like he was floating, his memory faded. He existed only in the present, only in sensation, and everything else was meaningless. In those periods of heady intoxication he barely remembered his own name.

He dozed, and sometimes he cried and sometimes he drifted, but it was never enough to forget his stimulation. It was like torture. His cock was almost painfully hard. He wanted to fuck or be fucked, and even his drug-addled mind was astonished he no longer cared about distinguishing between the two.

He guessed Alysia was similarly bound in a crate next to his, groaning and writhing at each bump in the road. The thought of her naked body, suspended like his, made Kynon want to scream with need. To taste her, to bite her, to fuck her. And then he cried again, because she was the sweet girl who had refused to kiss him behind the armory wall, and he was turning into something monstrous.

*****

The light hurt his eyes. Kynon shrank back into his bindings instinctively, but he recognized the smell and the rough hands of Captain Rennick and allowed himself to be brought gently to his feet as his eyes slowly adjusted to the light. The plug that had tormented him all day slid from his body as Rennick twisted it, and he sighed.

All around him he could see activity — men, horses, tents, and equipment. Kynon was standing, naked and trembling, in the midst of the mighty

Segasan army. He was surrounded by his enemies, and he had been humiliated, despoiled, and enslaved. As he watched, a passing soldier grabbed lewdly at his own crotch and wiggled his hips. The men around the soldier laughed, and Kynon shrank back. His heart raced.

"Don't mind them," Rennick said, patting him on the shoulder. "They're just having a laugh."

Kynon shivered.

One tent stood out from the rest. Kynon recognized the crest on the canvas walls — the warlord's tent. How many times had he seen it from a distance and dreamed of sneaking inside to plant a knife in the heart of the fearsome warlord? It already felt like a lifetime ago. He wasn't a soldier or a prince now. He was less than nothing, and that was why the Segasans were laughing at him.

"Do you need to piss?" Rennick asked.

Nodding, Kynon allowed himself to be led around the side of the cart. It was more difficult than he thought; his cock was still hard, and there were men all around him. He flushed, embarrassed, as he relieved himself.

Rennick lifted a cup to his lips, and Kynon drank. The taste was already becoming familiar to him. "The procurators' blend," Captain Rennick told him. "Drink it all."

Kynon obeyed, regarding the captain fearfully.

Rennick took the cup back. "You can talk to me, you know, tribute. I'm not your master."

"What are you?" Kynon asked warily.

A smile split the captain's face. "I'm a glorified stable boy."

The captain led him into the warlord's tent and over to the central post of the tent. Two low couches protruded from the central post like the hands of a clock. Alysia was already lying on one, her wrists chained above her head to the post. She was restless, turning her slender body from side to side, her eyes closed, her thighs clamped together. Her torment, exactly the same as his, made Kynon immediately hard again.

He lay on the couch beside hers, allowed the captain to chain his wrists, and shuddered as the man ran a calloused hand across his abdomen. Kynon saw the captain's amusement. Perhaps he had intended the gesture as nothing more than the comforting pat one gave to a docile animal, but Kynon saw the small smile as he reacted to the captain's touch. The man's hand lingered for a moment, cool against Kynon's flesh, and then something that may have been interest passed briefly over his face and he left them.

Brasius entered the tent. He came and stood over his tributes, a quiet smile playing on his face. He knew exactly what the day of travel had done to them.

"Boy," he said. "Are you awake?"

Kynon snapped his eyes to Brasius's face, trying desperately to ignore his throbbing cock. He could feel the cool air against the head, and he knew it was already leaking. Like a dog responding to his master's voice, just hearing Brasius speak was almost enough to make him come. What the hell had that drink done to him?

"Master," he whispered, and the word sounded natural.

Brasius's smile widened. His eyes traveled Kynon's body and fell on his cock. "I trust you are not as reticent today, my tribute."

Kynon flushed with shame. "No, master."

"Open yourself," said Brasius. "You need a good fucking."

Beside him, Kynon heard Alysia groan in disappointment.

"Knees up," Brasius said, "legs open."

Kynon obeyed as he watched his master disrobe. The day before the warlord's massive cock had frightened him. It had hurt him. Today he didn't care. He wanted it inside him. He wanted it to finish the work of the plug that had tormented him all day.

"Oh gods!" He writhed as Brasius leaned down and gripped his cock. The warlord closed his fingers around his rigid flesh, and rubbed his thumb over the sensitive head. Kynon's hips bucked involuntarily, and Brasius laughed and released him.

"You don't get to come, tribute, until I am inside you."

Kynon wrapped his hands around the chains above his head and groaned.

Brasius knelt between Kynon's open legs. He put his hands on Kynon's knees, pushing them up so that Kynon's thighs were pressed against his body. Brasius leaned forward, resting his weight on Kynon's folded legs. Kynon groaned as the warm tip of the warlord's cock pressed against his anus, and shivered. He squeezed his eyes shut, willing himself to relax his muscles, and then realized that nothing had happened. His master was holding his position, teasing him with the feel of his cock. Kynon opened his eyes.

"Ask me nicely, prince," said the warlord.

"Please, master," Kynon said, closing his eyes again and hating himself. "Please fuck me, master."

Brasius answered with a thrust, and Kynon cried out as the massive cock entered him. There was no preamble, and it hurt. The plug had teased him. It had not opened him enough to take Brasius with ease. Possibly it would always hurt, Kynon thought, and that was why Brasius had chosen him for this pain and humiliation — a prince.

He struggled under Brasius's weight and felt tears squeeze out from under his eyelids. He had lost his erection.

He was surprised to feel a touch on his face, and he opened his eyes to find Brasius stroking his cheek.

"Hold still, boy," he said, his voice low. His eyes were almost black. "Breathe."

Kynon drew a shaking breath, forcing himself to stop struggling. "It hurts!"

"Breathe," his master said again.

Tears burned Kynon's eyes. He drew a deep breath and realized that the pain was not as sharp. It was more of an ache now.

"I am all the way inside you," his master said, and Kynon marveled at the way Brasius held himself still. He could see the tendons in the man's neck trembling with the effort. "Tell me what you feel."

"It hurts," Kynon whispered, closing his eyes again. His anus was too stretched, and every muscle inside of him protested at the intrusion of Brasius's cock. Then Brasius tilted his hips, and Kynon felt his master's cock push against that place inside him— that sensitive place that was somehow connected directly to his cock. His cock twitched, and Kynon gasped.

His master shifted position again, reaching down between their bodies to grip Kynon's cock in his hand again. Kynon arched his back. The pain in his ass had defused. Now it throbbed like a second heartbeat. His cock was immediately hard again under his master's touch, and he realized with confusion that the feeling was there again, and it was stronger than before: he wanted to be fucked.

He opened his eyes. "Please fuck me, master."

Brasius growled, releasing Kynon's cock. He pulled back. Kynon groaned, and Brasius thrust again. Kynon fought for leverage on the chains in order to meet his master's thrusts. Somewhere inside he was conscious of that fact that he was no longer a victim. He was an active participant. It didn't matter. He just wanted to come. More than that, strangely, he wanted to feel his master come.

Brasius thrust quickly, and Kynon pushed his hips up to meet each one. The feel of his master's cock inside him made his whole body throb. His cock was almost painfully hard. He wanted his master to fuck him even harder. He closed his eyes and arched his back, bending himself to his master's will. He pulled on the chains.

Brasius began to grunt as he kept up the furious tempo. "Come for me, boy!"

Kynon's body obeyed. His orgasm tore through him, and hot cum splashed onto his stomach and chest. His master held still and tensed and then bellowed as he came. Kynon felt the hot blast deep inside him. Brasius pulled out.

Kynon lay trembling on the couch.

Brasius leaned down and ran his fingers through the cum on Kynon's stomach. For a moment his fingers followed the path of the scar along Kynon's hip, and his eyes darkened again. Then he raised his hand to Kynon's face, and Kynon opened his lips instinctively.

"Good boy," said the warlord, inserting his fingers into Kynon's mouth so that he could taste himself. His breathing was still hard. "Good boy."

The hint of a smile tugged at the corners of the warlord's lips as he looked down at Kynon. His eyes were half-closed as Kynon sucked his fingers.

The look on his face was peculiar, and Kynon couldn't read it. On anyone else, he might have thought it was tenderness.

*****

In the darkness, Kynon listened to the sound of the warlord snoring gently. He tried to make himself more comfortable on the couch, but it was difficult to move with his hands bound above him. He saw light and squinted to try and make out the figure entering the tent. She came closer — it was Hera.

She unshackled Kynon and Alysia quietly, glancing up as she worked to be sure the warlord didn't awake. She raised a finger to her lips and beckoned them to follow her.

Every muscle in Kynon's body ached as he rose from the couch. Beside him, Alysia stumbled, and he caught her by the elbow to steady her. The warmth of her flesh from that one small contact made his heart race.

Outside, the camp was quiet. Low fires still burned as the night progressed toward dawn. Captain Rennick was waiting for them some distance away, standing in front of a tub full of water.

Hera led them to him. "Alysia, get in."

Alysia obeyed. Kynon saw from the look of relief on her face that the water wasn't too cold. She stood there, arms held out, and Rennick began to wash her.

Kynon, unsure what to do with himself, remembered Mistress Hera's previous instructions and lowered himself to his knees. He clasped his hands behind his neck, looking to Hera.

She didn't acknowledge him, and Kynon looked at the ground, ashamed. Had he expected praise like a trained dog? It wasn't his subservience that shamed him, he realized after a moment. It was that he'd wanted praise when every fiber of his being told him Mistress Hera would not applaud him for doing just what was expected of him. Her praise, he was sure, had to be earned. It frightened him that there was a part of him that wanted to earn it.

It was that damn drink, he thought. The procurators' blend. It had gone straight to his cock, messed with his head, and made him forget himself. It had turned him into a whore. Kynon felt tears prick his eyes.

Rennick tugged at his collar, and Kynon allowed himself to be pulled to his feet. He stepped into the tub, and Rennick began to scrub him down with a rough cloth.

"Bend over," the captain said.

Flushing, glad of the darkness, Kynon obeyed. Rennick swiped the cloth down between his buttocks and used his fingers to push it inside his anus. Kynon's cock hardened in response, and he flinched. Rennick withdrew the cloth and then reached around to clean his cock and balls. Kynon moved his hips toward the touch of the man's hand, and Rennick patted him on the back.

"Tomorrow you will be flogged," said Mistress Hera.

Kynon blanched, and Alysia gasped.

Hera smiled. "Rennick, take them back to their master's tent. He may wish to use them again before morning."

"Yes, Mistress Procurator," said Rennick and led them away.

Rennick stopped just short of the tent. He leaned close to Kynon's ear.

"Just a little pain," he said in a soothing tone. "Nothing more than you can handle."

Kynon tried not to sob as Rennick put his hand on his hip, rubbing gently.

"Please don't hurt us," Alysia whispered.

"You are tributes of the warlord Brasius," said Rennick. "You must submit."

Kynon nodded, shivering in the night air.

Rennick tugged on their collars. "Come now. Let's get you back to bed."

*****

It took Kynon a long time to sleep. He twisted on the couch, the chains around his wrists preventing him from lying comfortably. His shoulders ached, and the night was cooler now. He hated himself for what he had already become. He had been given to the warlord as a tribute, and he was honor-bound to obey, but he hated that he couldn't just remain passive. No, he'd raised his hips when the warlord had fucked him, letting the man thrust deeper into his flesh.

And he was afraid. Why was he going to be flogged? Wasn't it enough for these people that he had submitted, and submitted more willingly than they had any right to expect? What else could they demand of him? He didn't want to be a whipping boy for their crueler instincts.

His memory took him back to Caralis, to the first time he'd visited the brothel in the lower part of town. He had been with Nemic and Tolan, both of them eager to show their little brother a good time. The place was clean enough, the drinks came fast enough, and the women were pretty enough. He'd begged Conal to come with him, but Conal had got cold feet at the last minute. Kynon, just as nervous, hadn't dared back out, in case his brothers mocked him for it.

Then he'd chosen the wrong woman. She'd had at least a decade on him, and she had been more striking than beautiful. Kynon had chosen her because he didn't want someone young and conventionally pretty; he was afraid he might embarrass himself by performing badly. He had thought he wouldn't care if the older woman was disappointed in him.

"No, you mustn't choose Sylviana," Tolan had told him, red with laughter.

"Why not?" Kynon had asked.

Nemic had spilled his wine. *"Because she'll beat* you, little brother!*"*

"You're joking," Kynon had said, looking at them. He realized with sudden astonishment that they weren't.

"Oh no," Tolan had said, clapping him on the back. *"Whips, chains — the whole thing."*

"Do men pay for that?" Kynon had asked, wide-eyed.

"Don't knock it until you've tried it." Nemic had laughed and had steered Kynon toward one of the other women instead.

Kynon hadn't understood why anyone would pay to be hurt. What could it possibly achieve? He had discussed it with Conal the next day, speculating as to what Sylviana actually did to her clients and why they came back for more.

Conal had mused on it for a while, his clever blue eyes dancing. *"Maybe they are very important men who are very tired of giving all the orders. Maybe when she hits them, they get to feel insignificant."* He had frowned as he thought it through. *"Maybe they know* they should be ashamed of what they really want.*"*

"But who would want that?*"*

Conal had laughed at him then. *"Or maybe if you're so curious, you should have told your brothers to back off and gone with her yourself to find out if a slap on the face could make you hard!"*

It had embarrassed Kynon that there might be a link between the sexual act and pain that he had been too naive to consider. It was another thing for his brothers to mock. And even Conal.

Kynon thought back to the whipping he had suffered in the stable yard. It had hurt like hell. And then he remembered the sensation of the cold stone floor of his bedroom against the stinging welts in his back as he had come in the warlord's hand. It had been a strange mix of pain and pleasure. He had thought at the time that the pleasure had overcome the pain, but wondered now if he was missing the subtlety. Was it possible the pain had complemented the pleasure? Increased it?

He turned his head and looked up toward the warlord's bed. He could see the lamplight gleaming on the planes of the man's back. He slept on his stomach with one hand hanging over the edge of the bed.

Kynon hated him. But he remembered that hand gripping his cock. He remembered that handsome face contorted with effort as his master fucked him. He remembered the way his master's muscles rippled under his skin as he moved above him.

Kynon's cock twitched and hardened. He closed his eyes and tried to ignore the sensation, but it was too late for that. He groaned and bit his lip. If pain increased pleasure, did it follow that, in his case, his hate increased his desire?

Caught between arousal and fear, he prayed for sleep.

"Are you awake?" Alysia whispered in the darkness.

"Yes."

"I'm frightened," she whispered.

Kynon couldn't answer. He flushed and wondered how she could even speak to him when she'd seen the things that had been done to him. The things he had done.

"The drink," Alysia said. "It makes me…"

"I know," said Kynon miserably.

"And I like it," Alysia said, her voice fearful. "I want to be taken now, all of the time. What's wrong with me?"

"Me too," said Kynon. "It's wrong with me too."

*****

When Kynon awoke, it was almost light. The torches in the warlord's tent had burned low, and the tent was bathed in soft light. Outside Kynon could hear the sounds of the military camp waking to the new day, so familiar to him but now so alien. He was lying naked on the low couch, his arms chained above him. Three days ago he had been a soldier and a prince.

He could hear Alysia moaning. He turned his head and saw that Brasius was fucking her gently. He was astonished at the warlord's stamina. Alysia held her knees up as Brasius undulated softly against her. She moaned again, and Kynon felt her frustration as acutely as if it were his own. His cock stiffened.

He wondered how long Brasius had been fucking her. Alysia was flushed, her eyes closed. She was biting her bottom lip.

Brasius was teasing her, hardly moving when even Kynon could tell she desperately wanted him to thrust deeply. Her legs trembled with the effort of holding them up. Brasius shifted his position, holding himself up on his arms. He lowered his head and extended his tongue to lap at a nipple, and Alysia writhed.

"Please, master," she gasped. "Please fuck me."

Kynon's stomach clenched at the sound of her breathy plea. Had he sounded that desperate? Just hearing it, he wanted to be fucked again.

Brasius smiled at her and licked her breast again. She arched her back.

Then, abruptly, Brasius pulled out of her and rose to his feet. "Here is a lesson, girl. You come when I allow it, and now, my tribute, I do not allow it."

Alysia groaned and clamped her legs together. She rocked back and forth on the couch.

Kynon looked at the warlord in astonishment. His cock was hard, engorged, pressing up against his belly. The man's self-control amazed him.

The warlord crossed to Kynon's couch and leaned over to unshackle his wrists. "On your knees, boy."

Kynon obeyed as quickly as his aching

muscles allowed and clamped his hands behind his neck. He saw that his obedience satisfied Brasius.

"Please me," said the warlord, standing in front of him. "You may not use your hands."

Kynon fought with his reluctance. He was afraid to refuse, but the thought of a man's cock in his mouth disgusted him. He leaned forward, trying not to smell the musky scent of Brasius's cock. And of Alysia's cunt. He only hoped it would be over quickly.

He opened his mouth and tilted his head. The bulbous head of Brasius's cock passed between his lips, and Kynon tried not to let his disgust show on his face. He had watched Alysia perform this act. He reasoned that it couldn't be difficult, but once Brasius's cockhead was pushing against his tongue, he realized he had no idea what to do next. He was careful to keep use his lips to protect Brasius's cock from his teeth. He flicked his tongue tentatively against the warm cockhead, feeling the tip glance across the slit at the end. The growl that escaped Brasius convinced him he was doing something right, so he did it again.

Brasius's cock tasted strange. Not horrible, but strange. Salt and sweat and musk. And it pulsed under his tongue, a living thing.

He felt his master's hands in his hair, pulling him forward.

Kynon tried not to panic as Brasius pushed his cock farther into his mouth. He felt the head press against the back of his throat and realized he couldn't breathe. He tried to pull back, but Brasius tightened his grip on his hair.

Kynon tried to suck in breath. He hollowed his cheeks and felt Brasius's cock twitch. Then Brasius allowed him to draw back for a breath. Kynon sucked in air as Brasius's cock filled his mouth again. He grew dizzy as Brasius began to thrust into his mouth, and he tried desperately to time his breaths correctly. He was afraid he'd choke. Then Brasius began to thrust faster, a staccato burst. Kynon felt him stiffen, and then his mouth and throat were flooded with hot cum. He swallowed it as quickly as he could, feeling some dribble out of the corners of his mouth.

Brasius released him, and Kynon leaned back, gasping heavily. He licked his lips before he could stop himself. He had tasted his own semen, after all, and Brasius's was much the same.

Brasius leaned down and pulled him to his feet. "Well done," he said, his breaths coming fast. He stroked Kynon's cheek. Kynon stared at the groundsheet, ashamed because he found himself leaning into the tender touch. "Good boy."

Kynon did not sleep for a long time. He could hear Brasius snoring gently on the bed. He twisted and turned on the low couch, his cock tormenting him, and listened to Alysia's frustrated sighs from close by.

*****

When he was next released from the crate, Kynon saw that the landscape had changed. They were in a field this time. Empty cottages lined the ridge overlooking the camp, and farther back, Kynon saw woodlands. This countryside, fertile farmland, had been abandoned in the face of the warlord's army. It must have been part of Caralis, Kynon thought, but he didn't recognize it. Even the horizon was made unfamiliar by the warlord; fearsome siege engines were silhouetted against the sunset.

Rennick led him to the smaller tent. "You'll be trained here," he said and pushed him inside.

Hera was waiting for him.

Kynon went to his knees immediately, clasping his hands behind his neck. His gaze fell on a strange device in the middle of the tent. It was a platform made of two padded leather sections. There were iron rings set into the sides.

Kynon fought off a rush of panic. This was it. This was what he had been dreading. He wanted to run. His rational mind knew he wouldn't get far, that he would be caught and punished, but he was frightened. The memory of his whipping at Rennick's hand was still fresh, and he couldn't bear the thought of it happening again. To comply meant pain. To run meant pain. He trembled.

"Come here."

Kynon stood, shaking, and allowed Hera to position him on the platform. His knees rested on one section, and then Hera bent him forward so that his chest pressed against the other section. Hera angled it so that he was comfortable.

"Knees apart," she said.

Kynon obeyed, his stomach twisting as she fastened leather cuffs around his ankles. He heard the slither of chains as the cuffs were attached to the rings on the platform and pulled tight. His wrists were then similarly restrained.

Hera placed her hand against the side of his ribs, feeling his shallow breaths and his thumping heartbeat. "You will learn to trust this."

Kynon swallowed.

Hera moved in front of him and opened a small trunk. She withdrew something. "This is a flogger. Look at it."

Hera held out the flogger; a dozen or so thin strips of leather sprouted from a carved handle. The leather tails were only short, and Kynon understood immediately there was no way they could cause the sort of pain he'd suffered at Rennick's hand back in the stable yard at Caralis. The flogger would sting him, but he hoped it would not cut his flesh.

She moved around behind him and ran the tails over his back. They were soft. Kynon was relieved by that, even as he tensed in anticipation.

"You are afraid," Hera said.

Her voice sounded sympathetic.

"That it pleases your master to have you flogged is enough of a reason to submit willingly," Hera said, "but you will find that a small amount of pain increases pleasure."

Kynon gasped as she trailed the flogger down his lower back, between the cleft of his buttocks and over his balls. Already stimulated by his hours in the crate, his cock lengthened and stiffened.

"Good boy," said Hera, and he heard the smile in her voice. "When it hurts, you can take it. By the force of your will, you can make it feel good. Do you understand?"

"No, mistress," Kynon said.

"You will."

She thrashed the flogger across his back.

Kynon arched up and cried out. The shock, the pain. He struggled against his bonds, feeling tears in his eyes. But there was something else, something unexpected. His flesh tingled underneath the sting, spreading out in a wave to warm his flesh.

"Breathe into it," Hera said.

The second blow, as hard as the first, caught him across his spread buttocks and wrenched another strangled sob from his throat. Kynon jerked forward. He caught a breath and held it until the pain receded, and he realized with astonishment that his balls were tight and his cock was throbbing.

The third and forth blows came in quick succession, and Kynon began to tremble. The platform took his weight, and he sank into it gratefully. He heard himself moaning. He didn't know why it felt like this. He didn't know if he wanted it to stop or if he wanted Hera to hit him harder.

He lost count of the blows, concentrating only on holding himself together. He was afraid he would come. He was afraid he would lose his mind.

When Hera released him, he looked up at her with confusion and devotion, and she showed him a knowing smile.

"That's enough for your first time, tribute. You have done well." She helped him stand. "You may thank me."

"Thank you, mistress."

"Your master will wish to see my handiwork."

Stumbling, Kynon allowed her to lead him back outside. The sunset had faded, and the dusk had softened into night. Rennick was waiting for him.

"Bring me the girl next," said Hera.

"Yes, Mistress Procurator," Rennick said. He walked Kynon toward Brasius's tent. "Shaky on your feet, tribute?"

Kynon was too dazed to answer.

Brasius was waiting for Kynon in his tent. He regarded him curiously as Rennick helped him onto his knees. Kynon turned his head as he heard the captain leave with Alysia, and then closed his eyes.

His entire body was radiating heat. His skin was on fire, and his whole body throbbed. His master moved around behind him, and then Brasius's hands were on his back, tracing the web of stinging welts Hera had left him.

"How do you feel, tribute?" Brasius growled

into his ear.

Kynon sighed as his master's hands explored his burning flesh. "Fire."

Brasius laughed, kneeling behind him. "Are you hard, tribute?"

"Yes, master," Kynon said.

Brasius parted his buttocks with his hands, and Kynon felt his master's thick cockhead rubbing against his anus. The cockhead was damp with fluid and hotter than his own burning flesh. He wanted it inside him. Kynon pressed back, feeling the cockhead push past his ring of muscle. The pain increased the pleasure; shuddering and jerking, unable to stop himself, Kynon came as Brasius entered him.

"Oh gods!" Kynon cried out, his muscles spasming.

Brasius slipped an arm around his neck, holding him upright. "You're not supposed to come, tribute, until I say."

"I'm sorry, master!" Kynon managed.

He squirmed as Brasius slid his other hand down his stomach, and then the warlord's fingers curled around his wet cock. "A procurator would punish you for that."

Kynon heard the smile in the warlord's voice and gasped for breath as his master tensed the arm around his throat. Shifting suddenly, Brasius thrust and impaled Kynon with his cock.

"You won't come again, will you, tribute?"

"No, master," Kynon gasped, feeling

Brasius's hand tighten around his cock. He groaned. Brasius wanted to make a liar out of him, and Kynon wanted to let it happen.

Brasius began to fuck him slowly.

His master's arm was like a vise around his throat. Kynon struggled to breathe. His tormented cock felt as hard as stone in his master's fist. He wondered desperately what would happen first: would he come, or would he suffocate? He tried to struggle, but Brasius was too strong for him.

Kynon grew dizzy. At the last moment Brasius's hold on his throat relaxed, and Kynon gasped for breath. In that same instant Brasius began to fuck him harder. His entire body shaking, Kynon tried desperately to remain still. He wanted to escape the warlord. He wanted to come. He couldn't tell which one he wanted the most.

Brasius froze, his cock swelling inside Kynon's pulsing flesh. Brasius grunted, jerked upward, and came. He gripped Kynon's cock tightly as he did, and Kynon cried out with the effort of not coming.

Brasius pulled out of him, panting. "Did you come, tribute?"

Kynon fell forward. "No, master."

"Remember this lesson tomorrow, when you're so hard it hurts. Understand?"

"Yes, master," Kynon said miserably.

Brasius pointed to the couch.

Kynon didn't have the energy to climb to his feet, so he crawled instead. He pulled himself up onto the couch with difficulty and allowed Brasius to chain him. He scowled as Brasius stood above him, smiling at his stiff cock.

"Something to say, tribute?" Brasius asked him. He raised his eyebrows, waiting.

Kynon fought with the temptation to spit every invective he'd ever heard at the man. For enslaving him, for fucking him, and worst, for refusing to let him come.

"No, master," he managed.

Brasius only shook his head. "Where's that fire now, tribute?"

*****

The days and nights began to bleed together. In the middle of the night, bound over a padded platform in what he had come to think of as the training tent, Kynon couldn't remember if it was the third of fourth time he was going to be flogged.

He clenched his buttocks in anticipation as Hera moved around behind him. Like always, she surprised him. She landed the flogger on his shoulders instead, and Kynon cried out at the sudden sting. Underneath the pain, warmth spread throughout his flesh. He still didn't understand how it hurt and felt good at the same time. It was almost like pulling a scab, except *that* had never made his cock hard.

He hated this, he was afraid of this, and he loved this as well. What the hell was wrong with him? The anticipation, the humiliation, the pain, and the throbbing heat. Kynon only knew that once the flogging was over, he hoped his master fucked him. He wanted to be lying on his back, his master's cock inside him, every thrust pushing him against the couch and reigniting the wonderful sting in his back.

Hera recited the rules for him between the stinging lashes, and it was as though she were branding them into his flesh:

"You will assume the position."

"You will not speak unless it is to answer a question."

"You will not come without permission."

"You will obey."

The hardness of his cock pleased Mistress Hera when she reached around under him to feel it. Her cool fingers stroked its length, and Kynon gasped.

She straightened again. "You are learning fast, tribute. You may thank me."

"Thank you, mistress," he gasped.

This had become his routine. During the days he was kept in the crate, suspended and plugged, and in the evenings he was chained in his master's tent for his master to use as he pleased. When Brasius slept, Hera came to fetch the tributes, and their training began. By dawn they would be back in the tent, and Brasius would inspect the marks on their bodies and perhaps take them again.

Kynon could no longer distinguish pain from

the anticipation of pleasure. When the flogger hit his tender skin, it was as if Brasius were already fucking him.

Alysia was similarly restrained on a platform beside him. Kynon could hear her breathing. Every gasp and moan made him harder.

He heard the whistle of the flogger and tensed, but this time it was Alysia who cried out.

"You may thank me," Hera said dispassionately.

"Thank you, mistress," she gasped.

The floggings were gentle. Hera had never broken their skin. She worked the flogger expertly, from their thighs up to their shoulders, inflaming their flesh. They trusted her and trusted the pain. Kynon realized, as Hera ran her cool fingers down his burning flesh, that a part of him never wanted the strange journey to end.

*****

The next evening when he was released from the crate by the captain, Kynon was almost crying. The rocking webbing and the unyielding plug had kept him hard all day. If he could just move, if he could just touch himself, but release had been impossible. His cock was painfully hard. As the captain helped him to his feet, it rubbed against the other man's leggings, and he almost came then and there.

Captain Rennick, sensing the urgency,

pushed him away quickly. "Watch yourself, tribute." His face softened. "Come on. You will eat in the main tent."

Kynon looked at him in surprise.

Brasius and his trusted commanders ate in a separate tent. The luxury of the military camp surprised Kynon, but he supposed if you had made a life out of war, there was no reason not to make it as comfortable as possible.

Inside the tent Kynon saw the other tributes for the first time since Caralis. They were all naked and collared, and they all looked at one another with shameful faces. Brasius, Kynon saw, was the only man with two tributes. He and Alysia were chained to either side of Brasius's chair and seated on the groundsheet of the tent.

Servants walked around the circled chairs, offering food to the warlord and his men. There were no tables in the tent. There was nothing to hide the tributes from one another.

Kynon looked at the ground to avoid looking at the other tributes. They had been the privileged sons and daughters of noble families. Now they were slaves, fucked any which way at the pleasure of their masters. And Kynon had been a prince, a leader. But their real shame, Kynon guessed, was that they were learning to like it. He was still hard from the undulating journey in the crate, and a quick glance around the tent showed him that he wasn't the only one.

Arron was sitting almost directly opposite

and Kynon hardly recognized him. It was as though someone else were wearing his face. Arron was trembling, Kynon saw, and there was fear in his eyes. But there was also something else, something that wasn't fear. It was desire, and Arron battled with it. Kynon knew that contradictory need. He felt it now like a punch to the guts, and stared at the ground again.

The tributes ate when their masters remembered to feed them. Kynon opened his mouth obediently whenever Brasius touched food to his lips. His master was saving the fatty cuts of meat dipped in rich sauces for Alysia, and Kynon remembered Mistress Hera had said she was too skinny.

The warlord raised his cup of wine. "To Jorell!"

"Jorell!" the generals echoed.

Kynon allowed himself a small surge of pride at hearing that name. The warlord's second in command, his reputation as terrible as Brasius's, had been carried from the field of battle six months ago with the bolt of an arrow in his chest and a gash in his guts as wide as a man's arm. Caralis might have fallen, but at least they'd known that small victory first. Kynon savored the bitter taste of it for a moment and then remembered where he was.

Kynon had once known these men as enemies. He had studied their tactics and their strengths and weaknesses avidly, hoping to gain an advantage against them in battle. He had never imagined a day where he might be chained at the warlord's feet, listening to his enemies discuss inconsequential pleasantries like the wines of Segasa, the best place to hunt fowl, and some poet who was making a name for himself in the right circles.

The talk came around to the tributes in the end.

"She tries hard," General Wilkus said, patting his tribute on the head, "but she can't deep throat yet."

Wilkus, Kynon thought. Fifty years old. Cavalry commander. He led two battalions. He was nicknamed the Scourge of Santara. And his tribute was Renna, Lord Machin's youngest daughter. She had been due to marry, before Caralis fell. Kynon imagined her trying to deep throat Wilkus, and his cock stiffened again.

Animon laughed loudly. Thirty-eight years old, Kynon remembered. A brilliant tactician. The designer of the fearsome siege engines that caused the world to tremble. They called him the Destroyer of Cities. A native of Hallis, a small city-state that had fallen nine years before, although he had served the warlord for longer than that. He was a traitor to his own people.

As Kynon watched, Animon leaned down to feed his tribute. Kynon didn't know his name but recognized him as one of the sons of Deron, the head of the Merchant Guild. The young man's face was a picture of misery as he saw Kynon watching, so Kynon turned his face away.

"This one's shy," Animon said. "Except in the dark."

Brasius laughed as well. "They're simple folk, Animon! They think the darkness hides their shame."

"You know how I feel about shame," said Animon, and the whole tent erupted with laughter.

An old joke, Kynon thought, that was so well-known among friends that it needed no explanation. He had not expected to see such camaraderie among the warlord's men. Brasius showed his enemies no mercy. The whole world was afraid of him. Somehow Kynon had expected his generals to be afraid of him as well. He hadn't expected to hear so much easy laughter.

His master lowered his hand. There was no food in it this time, but Kynon opened his lips and took the warlord's fingers inside his mouth. They tasted of salt and sauces from the meal, and Kynon swirled his tongue around them.

He should have been humiliated, but instead his cock hardened as he sucked another man's fingers. His body had already learned the lesson: if he pleased his master, his master might deign to allow him some pleasure as well. He wanted desperately to be fucked and to be permitted to come as Brasius filled him with his cock.

"This one," Brasius said, jolting Kynon back into the present, "sometimes thinks he is still a prince."

Kynon blushed.

Brasius withdrew his fingers from Kynon's mouth and played them through his hair. Kynon leaned toward the touch. A week ago he had been a prince — a captive prince, but a prince all the same. Now he didn't recognize himself. He felt like he was losing his mind. He had become so focused on sensation and the promise of release that he could hardly summon a coherent thought. He was afraid he would be a shell by the time Brasius grew tired of him, if he ever did. The thought of his master growing tired of him frightened him. Disgusted at himself for forgetting the man was a monster, Kynon jerked away.

Brasius tightened his fingers in his hair and pulled him back. "Something to say, tribute?"

Kynon tried not to struggle.

Brasius uncurled his fingers and smoothed Kynon's hair. "Get between my legs if you want to use your mouth."

Trying not to cry, Kynon crawled between the warlord's legs. He raised his shaking hands to the ties on his master's leggings and fumbled with them for a moment before Brasius's cock sprang free. Kynon, his stomach clenched, moistened his lips with his tongue and took the head of the cock into his mouth. He closed his eyes and tried to pretend this was not happening in front of a tent full of people.

He ran his tongue over the slit in the head, and the warlord's cock jerked in his mouth. He laved it, swirling his tongue around the head and then underneath to find the thick vein. Brasius tasted of salt and precum, and Kynon's cock began to thicken. Then his master's hands were in his hair again, his fingertips rubbing gently against his scalp.

Kynon lifted his head and ran his mouth down the length of Brasius's cock. His master's pubic hair scratched against his cheek as his mouth found his balls. He felt them tighten under his lips and tongue and heard Brasius growl with pleasure. His hands on his master's thighs for balance, Kynon took Brasius's cock into his mouth again. The cockhead pressed against his palate, and Kynon adjusted his position, opened his throat, and took it in as deeply as he could.

Brasius began to thrust. He twisted his fingers in Kynon's hair, forcing him to take more cock. Kynon closed his eyes, sucking as strongly as he could. He couldn't get a breath now, but he could tell by the way Brasius's cock was jerking that his master was ready to come.

Kynon expected to feel the blast of hot cum in his throat at any second. To his surprise, Brasius suddenly pulled away. Kynon opened his eyes just in time to see the man's cock explode in front of his face. Streams of cum hit him, catching in his hair and his eyes, blinding him.

Brasius pushed him around to face the tent.

"This is your prince," he said scornfully. "Not so noble now, is he?"

The other tributes bowed their heads, and the generals roared with laughter.

*****

Back in the tent, chained to the couch and cloaked in darkness, Kynon wept. He was beginning to understand Brasius's need to humiliate him. It was because he was a prince, because he was a soldier, because he was an enemy that Brasius liked to see him brought down low. Kynon understood the humiliation, but it was the small signs of tenderness that confused him. In the dining tent, after he had despoiled his tribute, Brasius had taken a cloth and wiped Kynon's face and hair carefully. And he had made small comforting noises as he did so: *"Shh, shh, shh,"* until Kynon had stopped trembling.

Kynon didn't understand it. He could withstand any cruelty, he hoped, but cruelty followed by affection made no sense. It made no sense at all. He only knew it drew silent, strangled sobs out of him and kept him from any sleep at all.

Chapter Four: Subjugation

Blinking, half-blind from the darkness of the crate, Kynon allowed himself to be drawn out into the sunlight. It was the afternoon. Kynon felt the sun on his skin. It felt good, and Rennick allowed him to luxuriate in the warmth for a moment.

"No training today," Rennick said.

Kynon squinted in the sunlight. No training. He didn't know how to feel about that.

Kynon had lost count of the number of times he'd been fucked or flogged. They were like a dream to him now. He didn't understand how a flogging hurt and felt good at the same time. He didn't understand why he still struggled to submit, knowing he always would in the end. Knowing the pleasure was always greater than the pain and the humiliation. His subjugation was like a dream, and he couldn't escape it. He couldn't even tell if he wanted to escape it. Each day when the cart rolled to a stop, Kynon found himself almost breathless with anticipation. New pain, new pleasure — his eager body wanted it all while his mind struggled for understanding that wouldn't come. Kynon had learned to focus on sensation and let the days and nights pass over him. And now, when his rational mind told him that no training was a reprieve, he didn't know how to feel.

"Come on. Stop your daydreaming," Rennick said, smiling.

Rennick took Kynon to his master's tent, and Brasius pointed Kynon to his bed. Kynon glanced at his master's face, surprised.

"Go on," the warlord said. His face gave nothing away.

Suppressing a shiver, Kynon moved toward the bed. His bare feet dragged on the groundsheet. Kynon was used to his couch, which although it wasn't uncomfortable, came with the expectation of being bound and fucked. He had no idea what to expect from Brasius's bed. Kynon stood beside the bed, staring down at the thick mattress and the soft bedding. His throat was dry, and he fought to keep his hands from trembling.

Brasius gestured for him to lie down, and Kynon obeyed. How long had it been since he'd lain on a mattress? It sank under his weight. So soft. It was like floating. Kynon felt suddenly unanchored, almost dizzy, and gripped the side of the mattress with one hand. He could hardly bring himself to look at the warlord as the mattress dipped.

"Come here." Brasius lay beside him, still fully clothed, and opened his arms. Kynon, his heart thumping, slipped into his master's embrace. He lay his head against Brasius's chest, and his master closed his arms around him. It was a strange sensation. It was stillness and quiet. The warlord was embracing him, and he didn't know why. He didn't know what his master wanted from him.

"You are certainly one of the prettiest tributes I've ever claimed," Brasius said.

Kynon breathed in his master's scent. He smelled good. Like Rennick, Kynon realized — horses and leather and sweat. It was a masculine smell, a military smell, and Kynon inhaled deeply.

"You're not a prince anymore, are you, boy?" Brasius asked, looking down at him.

"No, master," Kynon said, but something that was almost defiance flared in his chest, and he dropped his eyes quickly.

But not quickly enough. Brasius gripped his hair and tilted his head upward. Kynon, expecting to see the monster's true face, felt his stomach flutter as the warlord kissed him instead. The intimacy of the gesture astonished him. He'd been on his knees and had the man's cock down his throat, but that was subjugation. This was tenderness, and he didn't know what to think of the monster when he was kind.

Kynon's lips parted as his master's tongue probed them. He took the tongue into his mouth willingly, letting his master claim him. His master tasted of wine. He moaned and felt Brasius smile. The smile grew until his master could no longer hold the kiss.

Brasius pulled his head away, looking into

Kynon's wide eyes. He was smiling, and his voice was low and amused. "How did that feel, boy?"

Kynon inhaled shakily. His eyes swam with tears, and he didn't know why. "Good, master."

"The pain you have suffered in these past few days," said Brasius softly, "has made you open to the pleasure."

"I don't understand, master," said Kynon.

Brasius brushed Kynon's lips with his own. "Would you have allowed yourself to like this a week ago?"

"No," Kynon whispered, his heart pounding. It was true. He had changed. How had they done it? Why hadn't he fought harder? Just because it felt good? It shouldn't have been enough to make him forget who he was.

"You must learn to trust the pain," Brasius said. "It will always lead you to greater pleasures."

"Yes, master." Kynon's throat ached. He wanted to cry. He didn't want to be this person. He didn't want to feel this way, and act this way, and beg for more every time they tormented him. But it was already too late.

Brasius pulled him closer. "Do you feel how hard you make me?"

The warlord's cock, still constrained by his leggings, pressed against Kynon's naked thigh. And he wanted it inside him. "Yes, master."

And there he was again, the needy tribute. His cock was hard and had been since his master had embraced him on the bed. He wriggled his hips, trying to find some friction, and Brasius laughed and held him still. His dark eyes danced. "Not now, boy."

Kynon sighed, disappointed, as Brasius released him and stood.

"You please me," the warlord said. His smile faded slowly, and Kynon watched the transformation breathlessly. The warlord's eyes grew darker and his jaw tightened. His face lost all expression and seemed more angular, more predatory.

He wants me, Kynon thought, and I want him. I wish he was dead.

Not because of Caralis, or because of war, but because Brasius was turning him into something he didn't recognize. He wanted to meet his master's lust with his own. He wanted to writhe underneath him, struggling against him and begging him and coming for him. He wanted it to hurt, and he wanted it to feel good. Brasius made him want to submit, to crave every indignity, and Kynon hated him for that. He hated that his heart swelled at his master's praise and at the hunger in his eyes. He hated that he wanted it. And he was so tired of always fighting his conflicting emotions.

The covering across the tent's entrance was opened, and Rennick appeared.

"Are our guests comfortable?" Brasius asked him, turning away from Kynon.

"Comfortable enough, sir," Rennick said. "And separated."

"Good," said Brasius. "Take the tribute."

Kynon cried out in dismay as the captain hauled him up by his leather collar. Had he done something wrong? Had Brasius seen the rebellion in his eyes? But Brasius had kissed him and said he pleased him. Brasius had *wanted* him. Kynon didn't understand.

He was hauled outside again. He fell to his knees in the dirt at the captain's feet. Rennick produced a length of cloth from the pouch at his belt. Rennick used the cloth to blindfold him. Then he bound his hands behind his back.

"Stand. Come on."

Rennick kept a grip on his collar as they moved through the camp. Kynon was afraid he would trip. His bare feet slipped in places, but he soon learned to trust Rennick's grip on the collar. Why was Rennick taking him away from his master's tent? What had he done wrong? And what was going to happen now? He tried not to panic as Rennick guided him.

He heard the *swoosh* of heavy fabric as they entered a tent and the heat of a fire somewhere close on his naked flesh. He was standing on a canvas groundsheet. Rennick applied pressure to his shoulders, and he went down on his knees.

"Here he is," Rennick said.

Kynon heard footsteps scuffing on the groundsheet of the tent. He turned his head to catch the movement but saw nothing through the blindfold. Then he heard the rustle of clothing in front of him, recognized it, and he opened his mouth obediently.

He only knew it wasn't Brasius. This man smelled different, and the head of the cock when it was pressed against his open lips tasted different.

Kynon took the cock between his lips and used his tongue to search for the slit in the end. This cock was heavy and tasted of salty precum. Kynon wished he could touch it with his hands, feel its length and shape, but his hands were bound. He drew it in gently, feeling it swell and harden and push against the roof of his mouth. Kynon adjusted his position, letting his tongue swirl around the head to find the thick vein underneath. The cock pulsed and trembled.

Kynon hollowed his cheeks and sucked, and the cock exploded in his mouth. Even as he swallowed, Kynon was relieved the man had come so quickly and not had a chance to thrust down his throat. That still frightened him with Brasius, and he trusted his master's experience. He didn't trust a stranger not to choke him.

"Take your time," Rennick said.

The man, breathing heavily, pushed something in front of Kynon and then moved around behind him. He pushed Kynon forward, and Kynon leaned his weight against whatever had been placed there. A chair? He hoped it would take his weight.

The man's touch was awkward, unpracticed. His fingers counted the knots in Kynon's spine, and then his trembling hands parted his buttocks.

"Wait!" It was Rennick. "Oil first, or you'll damage him."

Kynon frowned in worry. Would this unpracticed man hurt him more? He felt oil drizzled between his buttocks.

"Now use your fingers," Rennick said.

Kynon twisted and groaned as a probing finger was pushed into him, sliding past his defending muscles. The finger turned inside him, rubbing against the secret place there, and Kynon's cock leaped in response. He bore down against the finger and felt it slide farther in. It felt good.

"That's it, sir," said Rennick. "He likes that."

A second finger joined the first, and then a third. Kynon cock wept fluid as he began to move his hips.

"He's ready," advised Rennick, and the man removed his fingers and pressed his cockhead to Kynon's entrance. He hesitated, and Kynon groaned. The cock slid slowly into him, filling him and stretching him.

Kynon gasped. He lay his cheek against the chair as the cock pushed into him. He could hear the other man's heavy breath and feel his strength as the cock was fed inextricably into his body. He finally felt the man's thighs press against his buttocks.

The man paused then, and Kynon waited. When he finally began to thrust, Kynon couldn't prevent himself from moaning in pleasure. His cock, unattended, ached and pulsed, and he squeezed his muscles around the stranger's cock as the man picked up pace.

Kynon moaned and raised his hips to meet every thrust.

The other man came quickly. He froze, stiffened, and then his cock emptied inside Kynon's trembling body. It was too soon. Kynon groaned in frustration, his cock still hard. The man sagged against him, and he breathed heavily against Kynon's ear.

"I always loved you," he whispered.

Kynon felt his stomach twist. "*Conal?*"

*****

Afterward, when he was crying like he would never stop, Rennick returned him to Brasius, and Brasius took him into his bed. Alysia, chained on the couch, watched wide-eyed as Kynon wept.

"Because you think you're still a prince," said Brasius, straddling his thighs and holding down his arms.

Kynon wanted to be sick. He could still feel Conal's fluids leaking out of him. Still taste him.

"Because you call me master and you don't believe it," said Brasius. His earlier tenderness was gone now. His eyes were cold. He leaned forward, his face inches from Kynon's, and extended his tongue to taste his tears.

Kynon struggled under the warlord's grip even as he marveled at the man's strength. The torchlight made the warlord's naked body gleam.

"Because you need to learn your place," said Brasius. He got a knee between Kynon's thighs and pushed them apart.

"He was my friend!" Kynon managed, twisting back and forth.

Brasius caught both of his wrists in one hand and used the other to hold his face still. "Your friend? He was jealous, and ashamed, and all that other petty little bullshit you ignorant people torment yourselves with. His cock was hard the day Rennick whipped you."

Kynon arched his back as Brasius's cock entered him. He was still oiled and stretched from Conal, and he hadn't come all day. Brasius entered him quickly, smoothly, and Kynon squeezed his muscles around his master's cock. He loved the feel of his master's hard cock filling his throbbing ass, even when he hated his master.

Brasius kissed him, his tongue probing his mouth roughly. "You taste like cum, boy."

Kynon fought the urge to bite him and turned his head away. "He was my *friend*!"

Brasius gripped his jaw tightly and roughly twisted his head back again. "And I am your master! Look at me!"

Kynon's eyes swam with tears, but his cock throbbed as Brasius began to thrust. He tilted his hips to meet Brasius's thrusts. His cock was almost painfully hard.

"You will submit to me," grunted Brasius, slamming into him. "And you will submit to anyone I choose! That boy today couldn't agree quickly enough when I offered you, out of his father's hearing, of course. He's dreamed of your tight ass for years."

Kynon groaned, wishing he could block his ears to the words. "That's not true."

But gods, nothing else explained why Conal had taken him. He remembered the boy who had been his friend, the way Conal had been careless and reckless and had worn his heart on his sleeve. He had admired and envied that about Conal. He remembered the nights they'd drunk together, caused trouble together, and fallen asleep together. Had there been something behind Conal's eyes all that time that Kynon had never seen? He hated Conal. He hated Brasius. And he hated himself most of all.

Brasius reached down and twisted his hard nipple, and Kynon arched again. "Did it feel good, having your friend's cock inside you?"

Kynon gasped as Brasius thrust deeper.

"Answer me!"

Kynon shook his head. He couldn't answer. He hated himself for needing this, for craving the warlord's touch. He hated this unrecognizable thing he had become.

"Answer me," Brasius growled again. He caught Kynon's jaw again and twisted his head to face him. "Did it feel good?"

"What does it matter?" Kynon hissed. He tried to wrench his head free.

"Answer me!" Brasius demanded. He dug his fingers in, and Kynon flinched even as he raised his hips to meet another thrust.

It hurt, and Kynon's eyes stung with tears. The warlord was too strong, but Kynon couldn't stop struggling. He hated this, and he needed this. He didn't want to answer. He didn't want to say it aloud when the thought of it made him sick. He didn't want it to be real.

Brasius leaned forward and licked his cheek, and Kynon gasped and rocked against him urgently. "Tell me," Brasius growled in his ear. "Did it feel good?"

Kynon could hardly breathe as his tears began to flow. He wanted this. Whatever his master gave, he wanted. However low he sank.

"Felt good," he managed. Brasius nipped his ear with his teeth, and Kynon couldn't tell if his tears were from pain, humiliation, or relief. Brasius released his jaw and moved his fingers back down to his nipples. Kynon gasped and squeezed his muscles around Brasius's cock. The rest came out in a sob: "Not as good as you."

"Then come!" Brasius thrust again, and Kynon came. His entire body tensed and shuddered, his back arched like a bow, and semen splashed over his stomach.

"That's it," said Brasius, gasping for breath. "Good boy."

Kynon fell back onto the bed. Brasius's cock was still hard, still buried deeply inside him. It felt bigger than before now he'd come. Kynon trembled as Brasius thrust again, slowly and gently this time. Every nerve in his body sang, and he shivered. It was unbearable. He wanted it out, or he wanted it faster. He wanted something, and Brasius was hardly moving. Kynon writhed underneath him.

Brasius leaned down and kissed him again. Kynon opened his mouth, and Brasius's teeth caught his lower lip and tugged. Kynon gasped, and his stomach fluttered. Brasius's cock pulsed inside his stretched anus like a second heartbeat.

Brasius's lips moved over his jaw and down to his throat and nipped lightly. Kynon groaned and arched his head back to allow the older man his throat.

"Master," he whispered.

He twisted as Brasius licked at the beads of sweat that had caught in the hollow of his throat. Kynon groaned again, his cock hardening. He moved his hips, but Brasius growled, and he fought to remain still. The warlord's cock was impossibly huge inside him.

"Master," he whimpered, as Brasius tongue and teeth found his right nipple. He arched his back toward the exquisite pain, trembling as Brasius nipped and licked. "Oh gods, master!"

Brasius moved across to his left nipple. His hot breath gave Kynon gooseflesh, and he almost screamed when Brasius bit down.

"Shh," Brasius murmured. "Shh."

The pain was electric. Kynon's cock was fully

hard now, pointing to his stomach again. His whole body trembled from the warlord's attention. He thought he was going to come again without his cock even being touched.

Brasius pulled back and then thrust again, slowly and deliberately. Kynon tensed as his master's cock slid over that sensitive, needy place inside him. That place that sparked a fire in him.

"Master!" Kynon gasped, his voice ragged. "Please, fuck me!"

Brasius moved up to kiss him again. His voice was low, almost a growl. "Do you deserve it, tribute?"

Kynon wanted it and he needed it, but did he deserve it? He was a tribute. He didn't deserve pleasure any more than he deserved pain. His only duty was to willingly accept whatever one his master chose to bestow upon him. The realization made him shiver.

He whimpered. "No, master."

The warlord's face split with a pleased smile, and Kynon's heart skipped a beat. He was held on edge and he needed more, but just in that moment, that smile seemed like something new. A tiny connection that surpassed anything that had come before. It left him almost breathless, and then it was gone again.

"Good boy," Brasius said roughly.

He began to thrust quickly. Kynon raised his hips to meet each thrust. He kissed his master's lips willingly, gratefully, breathing in the scent of the man's sweat. He wished desperately that his hands were free so he could pull his master close to him, so he could feel him. But the moment between them had already passed.

Brasius looked him in the eye, commanding, domineering, the fearsome warlord again. "Come for me again, boy," he demanded, and crying with relief, Kynon obeyed.

*****

Ambassador Trefus and Conal must have traveled fast to catch the warlord. They dined that night with Brasius in the warlord's tent. Alysia had been sent to Mistress Hera for training. Kynon knelt on the ground between his master and Conal as they sat around the small table, hating them both, hating himself, and sunk in misery. He was sick of humiliation. He wished Trefus and Conal had never come and reminded him of how far he had fallen. He wished Brasius hadn't made him be here for this. He'd been almost resigned to his fate. He'd thought there was something in the warlord that wasn't entirely monstrous. Now it was like Caralis all over again. The shame was overpowering.

Kynon could see Conal's boots shifting restlessly on the groundsheet. He was agitated and couldn't hide it. Trefus had always said Conal would be hopeless as an ambassador. Kynon watched his boots scraping back and forth and tried not to cry.

"Here, you see," said Brasius. "I keep my tributes well."

Where was the man who had smiled at him? Brasius was already cold again. His voice was low and amused, gently mocking Kynon and the people who cared about him.

"That is a matter of some debate," said Trefus. His tone was mild, but his eyes were dark with worry. He shifted in his chair. "Your Highness?"

Kynon could hardly bring himself to look at Trefus. "Ambassador."

"Are you well, Your Highness?" Trefus asked him.

Kynon couldn't answer. He raised his eyes and dropped them quickly again. Bile rose in his throat. He wanted to be sick. And not just because he was kneeling naked in front of a man who still called him Highness. He hardly noticed that humiliation. It took all his control not to fling himself at Conal and beat the living shit out of him. Conal hadn't conquered him. Conal hadn't claimed him. Conal didn't have the right to touch him like he had. He shuddered at the memory.

Brasius smiled. "You have embarrassed him, Trefus, but never mind. I like it when he blushes."

Trefus's mouth was a thin line. "I wish to hear him speak, my lord, if you please."

Brasius raised his brows. "Then frame your questions into those he can answer, Ambassador."

Trefus rose and moved around the table. He

reached out his hand to touch Kynon's shoulder, and Kynon flinched away.

Brasius shook his head. "He is fed, Trefus, and kept comfortably. We are even fattening up some of the skinnier ones. Tell him, tribute."

Kynon couldn't speak. He managed a nod.

"And his education is greatly improved," Brasius said. He laughed deeply, and Kynon flushed again. Why was he the one being humiliated here? Where the hell was Conal's shame?

Trefus's hand lingered above Kynon's shoulder, as though he were afraid to touch.

The warlord exhaled. "I know you are friends with Jaran, Trefus, and I know the king has his misgivings about his son's welfare, but you are a political animal first and foremost, and it is time to think of your own people. Caralis is Segasa's now. The same thing *will* happen to Lutrica. It may take me several years, but let's not pretend your armies are any match for mine. So you may report to your senate that they have two choices. They can either sign a treaty now, or they can wait until I march into the capital with my army at my back."

Trefus folded his hands into the sleeves of his robe and inclined his head. "If the outcome is the same, why not fight?"

Brasius smiled at that. "Because of the cost in lives. Because of the destruction to your lands and industries. And because I only take tributes from lands I conquer, not from allies." He looked at

Kynon. "Have you forgotten the position, tribute?"

Kynon looked at the ground, feeling tears sting his eyes. He clasped his shaking hands behind his neck.

"What are you doing, Kynon?" Conal blurted out, aghast.

Kynon glanced up and met his friend's eyes, and wished he hadn't. They were so full of pity that Kynon wanted to scream. *Your fault! This is your fault too!*

Trefus threw Conal a warning stare.

Brasius looked at Conal. "If I told him to, he'd suck my cock right now. He'd suck yours as well, if you like."

Conal's mouth dropped open.

Kynon bowed his head again, swallowing down the misery that rose in his throat. Brasius was teasing them both. He knew exactly what had occurred in that tent. The only man who didn't was the ambassador.

Trefus returned to his seat, sounding as calm as ever. "My lord, you don't need to debase a prince to prove your point to me. I will return to Lutrica and advise the senate of the options as you have presented them, but of course I cannot guarantee that they will listen."

"Of course," said Brasius. "I know how difficult politicians can be."

Kynon hunkered down, keeping his eyes on the ground and trying not to lift his head to smell the food. He was horribly aware of being between

Brasius and Conal. He could sense Conal's closeness, the stiffness of his posture. He was trying not to look at Kynon as much as Kynon was trying not to look at him.

Kynon hadn't known he had this capacity for misery. He'd thought the worst that could ever happen was being taken as Brasius's tribute. He had accepted the warlord had stolen his future, but couldn't have guessed he could steal the past as well. Every memory of Conal, of his friend, would be forever tainted by what had happened. And Brasius might have engineered it, but Conal had agreed. That stung the most.

"You keep a good table, my lord," said Trefus, "for a man who is always on the move."

"This food is the best Caralis has to offer," said Brasius. "It is the privilege of the conqueror to take the finest spoils." He dropped his hand and ran his fingers through Kynon's hair.

"You said, my lord," said Conal in a small voice, "that Kynon was to dine with us."

Kynon narrowed his eyes, and his whole body tensed. Who did Conal think he was, to be showing concern for his welfare now? He wanted to be angry. It felt better than humiliation. He tried desperately to hold on to his anger even as his shame crashed over it in waves and threatened to drown it.

"You may feed him if you wish," said Brasius. "I will show you."

Kynon thought he might be sick as he felt his

master's hand lift from his hair. A moment later it was in front of his face, a small piece of bread held between his thumb and forefinger. Conscious that both Trefus and Conal were watching avidly, Kynon lifted his head and opened his mouth to accept the morsel.

"Kynon?"

He could hardly bear raise his eyes to his friend. He couldn't speak.

"Kynon?" Conal's blue eyes were dark with grief and regret.

Kynon bowed his head again. Another word from Conal, and he knew he'd break. Or break Conal's legs. He didn't know which. If Conal had any sense at all, he'd shut his mouth. The last thing he wanted was for Kynon to start talking. It was all simmering there, just below the surface, just waiting to explode in tears and recriminations.

And maybe Conal sensed it too, because he suddenly turned on the warlord. "My lord, why do you take tributes?"

Without looking up, Kynon could tell Conal's face was flushed. Kynon knew him too well. Conal's voice, pitched slightly higher than usual, wavered despite all his efforts to the contrary. He was nervous, fully aware his sins could be laid out in the open in a heartbeat.

Kynon clenched his jaw. *Coward.* At the same time he remembered the boys they had been and could never be again, and his heart constricted. He was desperate to move, desperate to lash out, to fight, to scream, to cry, and it took everything he had to stay on his knees in an attitude of obedience.

He wished Conal and Trefus had never come. He might have been able to come to terms with his subjugation if only he hadn't seen them again. If only Conal hadn't touched him. He could have kept his past safe then and their friendship sacred. His memories could have been his consolation however low he had sunk, but now they would just be a new torment.

"The tradition of tributes is a long one in Segasa," Brasius told Conal. His tone was relaxed, his hand playing in Kynon's hair again. "It punishes men like Jaran who think they can stand against Segasa."

It was Trefus who spoke this time. "But Jaran was only defending his kingdom, Lord Brasius. He wasn't wrong to try."

Kynon thought he detected a hint of something in Trefus's voice. Was it confusion? The ambassador was too clever to let it show, but he must have sensed there was something here he wasn't being told. Kynon wondered if he guessed Conal was the cause of it.

"No," said Brasius. "He wasn't wrong to try. He was wrong to refuse a treaty when it was offered to him three years ago."

It was bad enough Kynon was kneeling naked at the warlord's feet, but was he expected to listen to the man tell lies about his father? The Segasan army had invaded Caralis despite all the king's efforts at diplomacy. Jaran had only ever wanted peace. The warlord didn't negotiate, because the warlord was a monster.

Kynon's chest swelled with anger.

"You're lying," he said before he could stop himself. When Brasius lifted his hand from his hair, Kynon braced for a blow, but nothing came.

Brasius regarded him stonily. "I have never lied to you, tribute. Your father refused a treaty."

Kynon shook his head. *Impossible!* He looked across at Trefus, but the ambassador didn't refute it. He couldn't even bring himself to look at Kynon, so of course it was the truth. It had to be. Kynon blinked back tears. Could he have been spared all this? He pushed the thought away. No, to fight had been their only option. He had to believe that. He had to, or otherwise his father had risked his life and, worse, his honor, for nothing.

"The sovereign is chosen by the gods to rule," he murmured. "There is no price too high to safeguard the crown."

Brasius smiled slightly. "A king is an accident of birth. He is no better or no worse than any other man."

Kynon's heart thumped loudly. He searched the warlord's face warily, wondering if he dared to respond. In that moment he forgot about Trefus and Conal. He forgot about his nakedness and shame. He only saw Brasius looking back at him and realized his master was waiting for him to speak.

"Am I to be the whipping boy for your

philosophy?" Kynon asked. His audacity frightened him. He was short of breath.

Brasius reached out and ran his fingers down Kynon's cheek. "No, tribute. You're to be the whipping boy for your own philosophy."

He said it with such strange tenderness that Kynon began to tremble. Brasius dropped his hand to the back of Kynon's neck and rubbed, and Kynon closed his eyes. It felt almost affectionate. Kynon tried to hate it and couldn't.

"We take tributes to punish men like your father," Brasius said in a low voice, "who think that the gods made them masters. We take their children, we enslave them, and we make them worship us."

He said it like it was inevitable.

It was too much. Kynon tried to keep his shoulders still as his misery washed over him and he began to cry, but he knew they were all watching him. They all saw him weeping like a child. And that was the point, of course. So that Trefus could report to his senate how he'd seen a prince of Caralis brought so low. And so could Conal, if he'd ever dare admit it to anyone.

"Kynon doesn't worship you!" Conal exclaimed abruptly.

Brasius tightened his fingers around the back of Kynon's neck, and Kynon tried to control his breathing. He heard the smile in Brasius's voice. "Do you want to see me prove it?"

"Don't," Kynon whispered, unsure if his

master could even hear him. "Please, don't."

Conal's seat fell back as he leaped to his feet. He stormed outside.

In the silence that followed, Trefus said simply, "They are friends."

Brasius raised his voice. "Rennick!"

The captain appeared instantly. "Sir?"

Brasius stroked the side of Kynon's neck. "Fetch the ambassador's son back here. Chain the tribute outside so they may speak freely."

"Yes, sir."

Kynon rose to his feet as Rennick tugged on the collar. His fear and shame overcame him. "Please!" He choked through his tears. "Please, master, don't! Master, please!"

Kynon saw Trefus flinch at the words, but Brasius was unmoved.

"*Please!*" Kynon couldn't bear the thought of being alone with Conal, not now. He struggled against Rennick.

Brasius narrowed his dark eyes. "Do you mean it, tribute?"

Kynon sagged with relief. "Yes, master! Please don't, master! Please don't make me go!"

"Then stay," Brasius said.

Kynon fell to his knees at the warlord's feet gratefully. He was crying again and pressing his forehead into Brasius's knee and murmuring his thanks through his tears.

"There, Trefus," Brasius said, "you may report that kindness to your senate as well."

Kynon didn't hear the ambassador's reply. He felt Brasius's fingers in his hair and closed his eyes. A part of him recognized that he should have been humiliated, but he wasn't. He was too thankful.

The warlord spoke. "Leave us. Go."

Kynon heard a chair pushed back as Trefus stood. He said nothing as he left, and Kynon wondered what he was thinking. He wondered what he would tell Jaran. *Your son was cowering at the warlord's feet like a slave. Like a dog.* Kynon shook with tears.

"You didn't know about the treaty," the warlord said in a quiet voice.

Kynon choked back a sob.

Brasius toyed with his hair as Kynon fought to control himself. "Why don't you want to talk to your dashing little friend?"

Kynon squeezed his eyes shut and shook his head.

"I meant it," Brasius said. "I would have let you."

"I don't want to," Kynon whispered.

The torches had burned low.

"How do you feel?" Brasius asked after a while.

"I don't know, master," Kynon whispered, afraid his voice would break.

Brasius lifted his hand from Kynon's hair. "Tell me."

Kynon's throat swelled. "He was my friend.

He shouldn't have betrayed that." He tried to marshal his thoughts. "It hurts, and I want to be angry."

"At me?" Brasius asked him.

"At him." Kynon swallowed. His muscles ached from kneeling for so long. He was tired. He didn't know how to explain what he was feeling and struggled to find the words. It was like they were wrenched from deep inside him, from a place he didn't want to lay open. His voice trembled when he spoke. "You're my master. You can give me to anyone you want, I know that, but he should have refused. He was my friend."

"Is he still your friend?" the warlord asked.

Kynon wanted to deny it and couldn't. He flushed. "I don't know, master."

Brasius was silent for a long time. He slipped his hand down to Kynon's neck and rubbed it gently. "You are full of surprises, tribute."

Kynon shivered under the soothing touch. So was the warlord.

*****

Kynon, sitting on the ground between his master's knees with his head resting against the warlord's thigh, opened his eyes when he heard the heavy *swoosh* of the tent door. He had been asleep, he realized. His body, aching from hard use and tears, had somehow relaxed enough under his master's touch to let it happen.

The torchlight gleamed in Mistress Hera's chestnut hair as she entered the tent. She looked at

Brasius and Kynon. "Commander?"

"Hera." Brasius's voice was low and calm. He ran his thumb along the outer edge of Kynon's ear.

Hera raised her eyebrows. "Commander, I am waiting for your tribute."

"Not tonight," Brasius said. "He is worn-out."

Kynon sighed in relief. He wasn't sure he could face the flogger tonight. He knew the pain could be cathartic, and he trusted it now, but he always fought a mental battle against fear and disobedience, and he didn't feel strong enough for that now. His catharsis, he thought, had been the few quiet words he had exchanged with his master before he'd fallen asleep. He didn't want to struggle again tonight.

Hera drew her brows together. "I hope you do not doubt my ability to train the tributes, Commander. My experience speaks for itself."

"I don't," Brasius said. "And it does, of course. But not tonight, Hera."

"Commander," she said, "he isn't even in the position!"

Kynon heard the rebuke in her tone, and so did Brasius.

The warlord's fingers tightened in Kynon's hair. "He's where I want him, Hera."

Kynon looked at Hera, hoping she would be pleased. She was regarding him with raised eyebrows instead, curiously, as though she had seen something that did not please her, but wasn't sure yet exactly what it was.

Chapter Five: Segasa

The lid of the crate had been left open. Kynon, rocking gently in the webbing, could feel the sun on his flesh. He felt more at peace than he had in days. Conal, his worst humiliation, had been followed by his best fuck from Brasius yet. His cock was hard at the memory. He could see the sunlight glinting on the bead of clear precum that leaked from his cockhead.

He closed his eyes, listening to the carters talking. Their voices were low and cheerful, and they lulled him.

The roads were wider now, smoother, but the plug in his anus was the largest yet. Every tiny jolt caused it to press against that awful, wonderful place inside him. It soothed and tormented him all at once. They had traveled through the night last night. Kynon thought they must be getting close to Segasa. The army had picked up pace. The men were more energetic, more eager.

Kynon thought he could smell the ocean. He could hear horses and men. He heard someone call out an order, and the cart rattled to a stop.

"You will look good with a tan, tribute," said the warlord, standing above him. He bent and began to unfasten Kynon's arms and legs.

Kynon rose awkwardly when his master gave him his hand, feeling the oiled plug slide out of him, and stood and looked out.

They were on a plain, a patchwork of farms and roads and fields and hedgerows. A few miles in front of them, low hills rose up. The hills were crested with towers and spires that gleamed in the sunlight. It was beautiful.

"Segasa," said Brasius.

Segasa. It was almost mythical. It was the place where his childish nightmares had come from. Everyone knew it was morally corrupt, decadent, and powerful beyond imagination. It produced armies that razed kingdoms to the ground. It had produced the warlord. It was the heart of his enemy.

Kynon had never seen a city so large. Trepidation caught him, and he shivered in the sunlight. What would happen there, when the strange journey ended? Could he be humiliated and despoiled any more? He didn't think that he could, but gods, that was probably just naïveté. Maybe there were a thousand ways left to torture and torment him. He looked at Brasius, wondering what the man expected of him.

"You may speak."

"I'm scared, master," Kynon whispered.

"Of what?" Brasius asked. He stroked

Kynon's hair.

"Of what will happen there," said Kynon. "I'm afraid I'll lose myself more."

Brasius smiled. "You ought to be afraid, tribute. I like it when you're afraid."

"Yes, master." Kynon shivered.

Brasius pushed him toward the end of the cart. "Go with the procurator. You are the star of my procession."

Kynon climbed carefully down from the cart and followed the robed procurator. He saw Alysia and the other tributes were already standing at the side of the road, being scrubbed clean.

Kynon held his arms out obediently as he was cleaned, dried, and oiled. His skin glistened. His wrists were buckled into leather cuffs behind his back and connected by a chain to his collar.

When the procurators offered him a cup of their blend, Kynon drank deeply. As always, it dulled his mind and went straight to his cock. The sensation of the cuffs and the chain down his back made him want to be more fully bound.

The tributes were loaded into another cart and stood there and waited while the army prepared to enter the city.

It took hours to reach the walls of the city. By that time masses of people had turned out on the streets to see the conquering hero Brasius return. Brasius rode at the head of his army, his cart of tributes behind him and his trusted generals behind them. The rest of the massive army, Kynon thought, would be lucky to make it inside the city walls by nightfall.

The city was amazing. Kynon had never seen so many houses, shops, and public buildings. He saw painted facades, fountains and wells, marble columns and steps, and roof tiles that gleamed in the sunlight. Segasa was vibrant, colorful, and stunning. Strings of flowers and streamers overhung the wide main street that twisted up the hill. People in the upper stories of houses leaned out of their windows and over balconies and cheered and clapped.

People lined the street, crowding in from the arterial roads. They cheered their hero, cheered his generals, and cheered the subjugation of the tributes. They threw flowers that the army trampled underfoot as the procession wound through the streets, heading up the largest hill toward the massive fortress there.

No, Kynon thought as it came into view — the citadel Mistress Hera had spoken of those long weeks ago. It was beautiful, its gates open to the rest of the city. It was made up of a massive central tower that twisted like a shell and gleamed like ivory. All around it, other towers and spires reached toward the sky as well, but none were as beautiful as the central tower. Flags and pennants fluttered in the wind. The citadel was as big as the entire capital town of Caralis.

Kynon was astonished. This was not what he had expected of a barbarian warlord.

The crowd at the citadel was huge. It met Brasius with a wall of joyful sound.

Kynon forgot his fear, looking around to take in as much as he could.

Their cart stopped at the entrance to the main tower, where soldiers in colorful livery held back the adoring crowds. Then the procurators advanced down the steps, each taking charge of a tribute. Kynon recognized the noble profile and chestnut hair of Mistress Hera long before she approached him and attached a thin silver chain to his collar.

Hera didn't speak, only led him up the stairs to the wild cheers of the crowd and into the main tower.

It was quiet inside the citadel after the noise outside. The hall was massive, bigger than any room he had ever seen. The sunlight flooded in through arched windows and gleamed on the marble tiles. The walls were covered in beautiful bas-relief scenes that shone with gold. Kynon had never seen such luxury.

Hera threw him a knowing smile, and he remembered when she had called Caralis a backwater. She had been right.

Kynon was anxious when he was separated from the other tributes and led up farther into the main tower. He saw so many staircases and passages leading off into all directions that he thought the citadel must be a labyrinth.

"You are dusty from the road," said Hera. "And thirsty, yes?"

"Yes, mistress," he answered.

"You will be cleaned first," said Hera, pushing open the doors to a massive, tiled room full of steam. The room was circular, and the tiles were hot underfoot. Kynon had read about such things once: rooms where the floors were heated from underneath by a system of furnaces. He had never thought to see such a place. In the center of the room was a large marble slab. Servants, red and sweaty, tipped ladles of water onto it that immediately dissolved into hissing clouds of steam.

"This is the warlord's tribute," Hera announced to the servants. "I expect your best work."

"Yes, Mistress Procurator," the servants murmured.

Hera left Kynon in the care of the servants and retreated back outside.

Kynon allowed himself to be led over to the marble slab. The servants motioned him to sit, and he did so, wary of the heat. The marble was warm, almost uncomfortably so, but he soon grew used to it.

"*Tch*," said an old man. "You are thirsty, yes? You must drink." He held up a cup of water to Kynon's lips. It was lukewarm, but Kynon drank anyway.

"If you don't drink, you'll shrivel up like a prune in here," the old man said and showed his teeth in a grin. "Won't look so pretty then, eh?" The old man unchained his hands and pushed him back onto the marble slab.

A pair of servants scrubbed him down with rough cloths while Kynon lay and sweat under their care. He was ashamed to see that the cloths came away so filthy. It was as though dirt was streaming from his pores.

A woman sat beside him on the marble slab and drew his head into her lap. Kynon flushed as she studied his face intently. She drew a razor out of a case and began to shave him carefully. Kynon closed his eyes, listening to the hiss of steam whenever water was thrown onto the slab. He felt like he was melting in the heat.

The woman shifted at last and knelt over him. Kynon watched as she began to work the razor gently between his pectoral muscles and down his chest. Kynon sucked in breath as she moved even lower, and tried not to flinch as the razor tugged at his pubic hair.

Another woman approached and raised his arm. She knelt on the tiles of the floor and began to shave his armpit.

He might as well not have been there. Kynon's ear, not yet attuned to the Segasan accent spoken at such speed, only caught every few words as the women nattered. It was enough to know they weren't talking about him. They were talking about some man and whether their friend was deceiving herself with him. Kynon was nothing to them.

Occasionally the old man passed, making his *tch-tch* noises at the women and offering Kynon more water.

Kynon was embarrassed. The woman working at his groin took hold of his cock and lifted it out of her way. She made some comment when he stiffened automatically, and the woman shaving his armpit laughed. Kynon squeezed his eyes shut.

Kynon didn't recognize himself when they were finished. His armpits, chest, and abdomen were completely bare. So was his groin. His cock looked huge against his bare skin. He gasped as he was doused in cool water, and then he was led outside to where Mistress Hera was waiting.

She looked him up and down approvingly as the servants reshackled him. "Come now. Follow me."

Kynon obeyed, leaving a trail of damp footprints on the tiles.

Hera led him up another set of wide stairs and down a passageway that was decorated with frescos. There was a grand set of double doors at the end of the passage. Hera threw them open.

"Your master's apartment," she said.

Kynon gaped when he saw it. The foyer, open and empty, led on to a second room. There was a large dining table there and a massive fireplace. The second room looked to be a study. Kynon had never seen so many books. Beyond the study was a bedroom, empty except for the large bed and a bureau. Wide windows looked out over the citadel and the city beyond it.

The final room was only small and covered

completely in tiles. Steps led down into a bath, big enough and deep enough to swim in, and it was filled with steaming-hot water. The sheer luxury of it took Kynon's breath away.

"You may wait here," Hera said, "for your master. Do you understand?"

"Yes, mistress," Kynon answered. He went to his knees with difficulty; his hands were still chained behind him.

Kynon wondered where Alysia was and why she wasn't with him. He was unused to being without her. They hardly spoke, but he missed her. A breeze sighed through the open window and cooled him. His tender flesh prickled.

It might have been hours before the door to the apartment swung open, and Kynon heard Brasius's familiar footfalls.

"Here you are," the warlord said. "All clean and pink. Are you hard for me, tribute?"

Kynon flushed. Just hearing the man's voice did the trick. "Yes, master."

Brasius leaned down behind him and unfastened his collar and his cuffs. It felt strange as they fell from him.

"Get in the water," said Brasius.

Kynon obeyed, feeling the heat work at his aching muscles. Brasius joined him and settled on one of the submerged steps, his back against the edge of the bath. Brasius ran a sponge over his body, and Kynon wondered if he should be doing that for him.

Brasius saw his questioning look and misinterpreted it. "Alysia is with the others, being prepared for tonight's reception," he said. "I wanted you with me."

Brasius looked at him expectantly, and Kynon lowered his eyes. Should he answer? How could he? He had no idea what sort of response his master was looking for. He studied the surface of the water intently and only looked up again when he heard his master rise.

Brasius curled his lips into a cruel smile. "I'm going to have your nipples ringed. The hot bath you've had will ensure it will hurt more."

Kynon's stomach twisted. He opened his mouth to plead and then closed it again. Obey, he told himself. He saw Brasius watching his face carefully as he struggled, and hoped his obedience might sway his master's mercy.

"Go and wait by the bed," said Brasius.

Kynon rose from the bath, trying to blink back his sudden tears. He could allow himself fear, but what was that feeling underneath? *Betrayal?* Stupid, because of course the warlord wasn't merciful. A few tender moments in all those long days of refined cruelty didn't mean anything. What the hell had happened to him that he'd forgotten for even a second that the warlord was a monster?

His master did not offer him a towel, so dripping, he entered the bedroom. Mistress Hera was waiting there with another procurator. She was holding a thick needle. Kynon felt his blood rush from his face.

He lowered himself to his knees and clasped his hands behind his neck.

"You will lie on the bed," Hera said, and Kynon rose again.

There was a piece of canvas draped over the bedding. Kynon wondered if it was because he was wet or because there would be a lot of blood. He swallowed anxiously but didn't resist.

He lay down and watched as the other procurator fastened cuffs to his wrists and ankles. The man fiddled with them, turning a mechanism at the head of the bed that pulled the slender chains tight. Kynon was unable to move. He was terrified. His master meant to hurt him for no reason and, worse, disfigure him. Why could he only ever find the strength to struggle when he was already bound?

Brasius appeared with a towel wrapped around his waist. He smiled at Kynon and sat beside him on the bed. "Proceed, Hera."

"Yes, commander," she said and bent over the bed. She took his left nipple between her fingers and began to pinch and worry at it until it stiffened.

Kynon screamed as the needle pierced his nipple. He tried to struggle, but the chains allowed him no movement. The sight of his blood made him want to vomit, and the pain was awful.

Hera poked the needle through and then pulled it free again. It was smeared with blood. She produced a gold ring and twisted it through the wound. Kynon cried out again, tears running down his face. He shook his head pleadingly as Hera began to pinch his other nipple.

She pierced his right nipple, and Kynon saw a flash of white. This time his body spasmed. His chest throbbed with pain, and he could smell his blood. Hera slid the small gold ring through, twisted it closed, and then wiped the blood away with a cloth.

Kynon cried. When his wrists and ankles were released, his first instinct was to hug his chest protectively, but he knew it would hurt more. He clenched his fingers into fists and rocked back and forth as he tried to expel the pain.

Brasius rubbed his abdomen gently and smiled at him. "How does that feel, boy?"

"It hurts, master," Kynon whispered.

Brasius leaned close to his ear. "I *own* you now, boy!"

He rose again, and Kynon shivered at the intensity in his eyes.

"Give the boy some blend, Hera, to take the edge off," the warlord said.

Hera raised her eyebrows slightly. "Are you certain, commander?"

"Do it," said Brasius.

Hera removed a flask from inside the folds of her blue robe. She pressed it to his lips, and Kynon lifted his head to drink eagerly. The pain dulled immediately, and warmth spread through him.

"You'll be the star tonight, tribute," Brasius

told him. "Once we get your new collar on you."

Kynon drifted.

*****

Kynon sat at his master's feet, Alysia beside him, as the citizens of Segasa came forward to congratulate the warlord on his victorious campaign. They admired his tributes aloud, as though Kynon and Alysia were nothing more than animals.

The great hall in the citadel was flooded with light. There must have been hundreds of dignitaries and even more musicians, dancers, and servants. Kynon had never seen anything like it. Massive chandeliers hung from the vaulted ceilings. The torchlight danced off the colorful frescoes on the walls, the marbled tiles, and the burnished gold detail in the cornices, arches, and columns. Light, music, and laughter welcomed the warlord back to Segasa.

Kynon and Alysia shone with oil. Alysia wore strands of gold twisted in her hair that matched her new gold collar. Kynon's gold collar shone too, and the rings in his nipples glinted in the light when he moved.

Alysia had been shaved as well. Kynon could see the oil glistening on her bare pubic mound. It made his cock hard.

Brasius and his commanders sat on a dais that overlooked the rest of the hall. They ate sparingly, Kynon saw, enjoying the company more than the food. None of them were gluttons, but the wine flowed freely.

Mistress Hera had a seat next to Brasius's. She seemed more relaxed than Kynon had known her. She talked to many people and laughed often. Her laugh stole the sternness from her noble face. She looked almost girlish as people commended her for the quality of the tributes she had chosen this campaign.

"I cannot take credit for nature's gifts," she smilingly told her admirers, "but I am pleased to take it for their docility."

Kynon remembered how she had promised him his attitude would be adjusted by the time they reached Segasa, and he lowered his eyes.

"Yes, Senator," Brasius said to one of the women who had come to speak to him, "I would have had the girl ringed as well, but she's a gift to someone else."

Alysia gasped, and Kynon looked up quickly.

Brasius saw them looking and only smiled.

Every so often their master bade either one of them stand so that they might be better displayed for his guests. Kynon watched as a man tugged on Alysia's nipples and inserted his hand between her legs to check if she was wet. Kynon was inspected just as thoroughly; a woman gripped his penis and rubbed the head of his cock with her thumb, laughing as he shivered and jerked his hips. It took all his effort not to come, and he was relieved when he was allowed to sit again.

The feast wore on long after the food had been served. Kynon had taken morsels from his master's fingers contentedly and tilted his head for sips of sweet, strong wine, but now he was dozing. His head was resting against his master's thigh while Brasius twisted his hair into elflocks. He was full, he was tipsy, and he was tired. The pain in his nipples stung him gently every now and then and made his heart beat a little faster.

"It hurts, master," he murmured, and Brasius twined his fingers in his hair.

Musicians played in the background. The hall shone with light.

Through half-closed eyes, Kynon could see the Animon, the Destroyer of Cities, leaning back in his chair while his tribute, on his knees between his master's legs, took his cock into his mouth. Nobody seemed surprised at the lewd display. Nobody even seemed to notice.

An unexpected touch on his shoulder jolted him out of his reverie. There was a man towering over him, his face red with wine. "Ah, Brasius! A fine tribute, indeed! Most fine!"

Brasius tightened his grip in Kynon's hair. "Yes, Senator, he is."

"Hands and knees, tribute," the man said, and Kynon shrank back as the senator began to handle himself under his robe. He fought off a shiver and steeled himself for what was to come.

"No." His master's curt voice surprised Kynon and evidently surprised the senator as well. The man gaped like a fish. "This is *my* tribute."

The exchange caught Mistress Hera's attention. She leaned toward them and lowered her voice. "What is it?"

The senator blustered, "It seems I have offended the warlord, Mistress Procurator, by preparing to use this tribute!"

Brasius dropped a hand onto Kynon's shoulder, and Kynon found himself encircling his master's calf with his arms. He squeezed his eyes shut.

"Commander?" Hera's voice was tense. "Commander, the tradition is clear!"

Brasius squeezed Kynon's shoulder gently. His voice was low. "My tribute, my rules."

Hera laughed, a clear, bell-like sound, but Kynon, his face turned to the floor, could tell her amusement was feigned. "Senator, you must forgive the warlord! Our journey was difficult and long. Perhaps another time."

"My tribute," Brasius repeated, "my rules. If you don't agree, Senator, you can find another man to lead Segasa's armies against Lutrica."

Kynon opened his eyes in time to see the senator gape again, execute a clumsy bow, and skitter back down the podium steps.

Kynon sagged with relief, even if he didn't understand what had happened. Brasius had given him to Conal, of all people, but he balked at the senator? A man who, going by the look on Hera's face, had a right to expect it? But he was relieved because he hadn't liked the leer on the man's face. He showed his thanks by pressing his face into his master's thigh gratefully and sighed when Brasius began to stroke his hair.

It was almost midnight when Brasius rose, bidding farewell to his guests and beckoning Kynon and Alysia to follow him. They trailed after him up the winding stairs to his private apartment.

"You pleased me tonight," he said as he unbuckled his belt. "Both of you. And I am reminded, Kynon, of a promise I made to you the first time I fucked you. Take Alysia, however you want, now, on the bed."

Kynon looked at his master uncertainly. "Master?"

Brasius was amused. "Tribute?" he asked in a teasing tone.

"I…" Kynon managed and then wondered what he'd been going to say.

"Go on, then." Brasius crossed the room and settled himself into a chair to watch.

Kynon was struck with unexpected shyness. He had no idea how to proceed with Alysia. He glanced at her face and saw she was looking at him with wide eyes. She reached out, took his hand, and drew him close to the bed.

"I want you," she said.

"Like this?" he asked her.

"Yes," she said and reached down and

stroked his cock.

Kynon lay her back on the bed, and she opened her legs for him. Like him, she was always ready. He slipped his hand between her thighs anyway, watching her bite her lip, to check she was wet. He slipped his fingers to her inner lips and worked between them. Her cunt was warm and hot and gripped his fingers as he pushed them into her. He slipped them out again and moved his hand upward to find the small node of flesh there. He caught it between his fingers. Alysia shivered.

He leaned down to kiss her; her lips were soft and tasted like wine. Their tongues met.

Kynon took his cock in his hand and worked the head up and down her slit until he felt it notch into place. He held her by the hips and pushed into her. Her inner muscles drew him in smoothly.

How long had it been, he thought, since he'd been the one fucking instead of being fucked? It felt like years. He only knew that the last time he'd done this it hadn't been with anyone as beautiful as Alysia, and he hadn't cared if she came or not. He wanted to make Alysia moan and shudder the way she did under Brasius.

He lowered his head to taste her nipples. Alysia moaned and wrapped her legs around him, catching his hair in her hands. Kynon began to thrust; Alysia matched him. He moved his head up to find her jaw, her throat, her lips, and she turned her head and caught his earlobe in her teeth.

Alysia! This was Alysia! This was the girl

he'd loved and who had refused him a kiss all those years ago. Kynon had spent years fantasizing about her, fumbling alone in the dark, but his adolescent dreams hadn't been this vivid, this wanton. This was better than he had ever imagined.

Her erect nipples brushed against his, catching in the rings, and the sudden flash of pain made Kynon's cock leap inside her.

Alysia came, her cunt gripping his cock tightly. He felt it fluttering around his flesh and came as well, the muscles inside her draining his cock. He fell forward onto her, and she kissed his mouth, his eyelids, his jawline.

Kynon had almost forgotten Brasius was there until his master's hand stroked his sweaty back gently. "You may thank me for my kindness."

"Thank you, master," Kynon said. He stood and accepted his master's kiss.

"Thank you, master," said Alysia, attempting to rise.

"No," said Brasius. "You stay right there."

He took Kynon by the collar and led him to the foot of the bed. Kynon knelt, and his master attached a chain to the collar. There was a thick rug on the floor that Kynon hoped would keep him warm.

He lay down on his side, listening to Brasius fucking Alysia and wondering which one of them he envied the most.

*****

Later, listening to his master's light snores, Kynon heard Alysia's chains slither as she shifted.

"You were good," she said, her voice low with embarrassment. "I just wanted to tell you that. I wanted you to know."

It was odd that they could still feel shame, Kynon thought.

"You were good as well," he said. "*We* were good."

He heard the smile in her voice. "Maybe he'll let us do it again. Your rings, how do they feel?"

Kynon blushed. "They feel strange."

"Did it hurt?" she whispered in the darkness.

"It hurt like hell," Kynon whispered back. "But it feels better now."

He flushed. It felt more than better. The gentle throbbing pain in his nipples, brought alive with every heartbeat, echoed in his cock.

"He likes you more," Alysia said.

Kynon felt a jolt of surprise. "He uses us."

"I've seen how he looks at you," Alysia said. "Like he could devour you. I asked Procurator Loran if he preferred men to women, and he said not until you."

A glow spread through Kynon's belly, and he tried to ignore it. Brasius didn't like either of them. He used them, and it just happened they had been trained to like it. If he fucked Kynon more, it was only because it pleased him to humiliate the son of a king. It had nothing to do with his personal preferences or with Kynon personally. Part of his mind seized hopefully on Alysia's words, wondering if it explained what had happened at the reception, but he couldn't believe it. This was the warlord, and the warlord was a monster.

"I don't want to be a gift to anyone else," Alysia said.

"I don't want you to go," Kynon whispered back.

"I'll miss you," Alysia said, and she sounded very afraid.

Kynon wished that their chains were long enough to allow them to touch hands.

Chapter Six: Separation

On his first morning in the citadel, Kynon awoke slowly. He could feel sunlight from the wide windows against his naked back, and he luxuriated for a moment in the warmth. He opened his eyes and realized Alysia was not chained beside him. He looked up and found Captain Rennick standing over him. The captain crouched when he saw Kynon was awake.

"She's not gone yet," he said in a voice barely above a whisper. "She's in the bath."

Rennick always seemed to know exactly what he was thinking. Kynon was about to ask why he was whispering, when he became aware he could hear voices coming from the study.

He looked at Rennick, wide-eyed, and Rennick raised a finger to his lips.

"Completed his training?" It was Mistress Hera, and her voice was arch. "I disagree! I have hardly begun!"

Brasius said something pitched too low for Kynon to hear.

"Commander, I am chief procurator. It *is* my

responsibility. What happened last night reflected on me!" Her voice grew hard. "I do not want to have to put this before the senate, my lord, but I will. My authority is quite clear in this case."

Kynon's breath caught in his throat. Brasius and Hera were arguing about him! He could feel his heart thumping wildly and struggled to catch Hera's words.

"But he isn't just your tribute, Commander," she said firmly. "He is Segasa's tribute."

Rennick sensed their movement before Kynon did. He stood again and looked straight ahead as Mistress Hera swept out of the study, her blue robes flowing behind her. Kynon feigned sleep.

"Rennick," said Mistress Hera. "The tribute *will* continue his training!"

"Yes, Mistress Procurator," Rennick said blandly.

She slammed the door to the apartment after her when she left.

Kynon was relieved Hera would continue to train him. Something in him craved the structure of the training sessions. They were his only certainty in an increasingly strange existence. And he trusted Hera, even though she had been the one wielding the needles the night before. Or maybe even because of it. Hera had only hurt him as much as the task required, and Kynon could appreciate that.

Kynon opened his eyes again in time to see Brasius walk in. He looked tired, and Kynon was surprised. He'd never seen the warlord show any weakness. He was even more surprised at the slight smile Brasius showed him when he saw that he was watching.

"Good morning, Rennick."

"Good morning, sir," Rennick said.

"Where is Alysia?" Brasius asked.

Rennick nodded toward the bathroom.

Brasius sat on the bed and yawned. "I'm getting too old for late nights, Rennick."

Rennick laughed as he bent to unchain Kynon. "I don't think so, sir!"

Kynon rose to his feet, his muscles aching, and moved around to the side of the bed. He was about to go to his knees when Brasius held up a hand to stop him and drew him down onto the bed beside him instead.

Kynon relaxed as his master put an arm around him and pulled him into a gentle embrace.

"Good morning, tribute," Brasius said, his voice low against Kynon's ear.

"Good morning, master," Kynon whispered back.

"That wasn't a question," Brasius said, and Kynon felt a rush of panic that he'd broken a rule, before he realized his master wasn't correcting him for responding. Was he testing him? Was he *teasing* him?

Kynon swallowed. He wasn't sure what his master expected of him, and he was frightened he would make a misstep. He understood the rules, trusted them, and now, sensing there was something new at play, Kynon was anxious. This was uncharted territory.

Brasius saw the trepidation in his face and smiled slightly.

Kynon looked up when Alysia appeared from the bathroom. She was combing the tangles out of her wet hair.

She reminded Kynon of a fresco he had seen the night before on the way to the reception: a water nymph, rising from the river, her golden hair flowing around her like silk. Except the water nymph had been pale. Alysia was pink and glowing from the hot bath. She turned, and Kynon saw faint welts across her buttocks. He wanted to touch them and looked away instead. He found himself remembering the night before with a mixture of shame and longing — the feel of her nipples snagging against his rings and the way she had cried out when she came.

Brasius tightened his arm around Kynon's shoulders briefly.

"Today is Alysia's last day with us," Brasius told him. "Let us go to the training rooms."

Rennick chained them and led them outside.

Kynon saw Rennick had a real spring in his step. He was glad to be home, obviously, surrounded by things that were familiar. It was all alien to Kynon. He had grown up in a small town, in a castle built out of dark stones where cold wind blew off the river.

The citadel was different. The walls were

covered in smooth, light plaster. Many of them had been decorated with frescoes depicting Segasa's history and traditions. Kynon's gaze slid over the colorful scenes as he passed them. He saw harvests, heroes, parades, battles, and riches, but he didn't understand the significance of the people and events the frescoes depicted. He didn't know the history of Segasa. He had only been told what he had needed to know: Segasa was the enemy of Caralis, and it had created the unstoppable warlord Brasius.

He had not expected Segasa to be beautiful. Every passageway and wall of the citadel was filled with light; there were windows everywhere that opened to the light breeze and the sun. The citadel was beautiful and intimidating.

Rennick led Kynon and Alysia down a set of wide, shallow steps. They exchanged glances as they followed the captain and their master. Kynon hoped his eyes conveyed everything he was thinking: *I hope you won't be afraid. I hope you will be treated kindly. I will miss you.*

"The training rooms," Rennick said over his shoulder as they arrived in an airy passage with closed doors on either side. Brasius opened one of the doors.

Kynon hadn't known what to expect. A variation on Mistress Hera's tent, he supposed, but there were no platforms, no shackles, and no instruments of ecstatic torment on the walls. There was something hanging from the ceiling. Kynon saw a jumble of leather straps hanging unused and shapeless and didn't understand what he was looking at until his master and Rennick began to separate the straps.

It was a harness.

Once he had been buckled into it, the harness reminded Kynon of those days he had spent traveling in the crate. He was lifted from the ground, supported under his arms, his torso, and his knees. The chains on the harness were adjustable. At the moment he was held parallel to the floor, but he knew his master could easily tilt him any way he chose. To be totally in his master's power in this way made his cock hard; a happy coincidence, he supposed, or had the procurators back in Caralis been searching for something more than youth and good looks? Had they seen something in him that he hadn't even known was there? Maybe there was a part of him that had always wanted to be subjugated.

Alysia was suspended in a second harness just out of his reach. Her legs were splayed and Brasius had inserted a pair of carved marble phalluses into her orifices. Kynon had never wanted to fuck her more than when he saw her like that, mewling her need like an animal.

Brasius moved around behind Kynon, and Kynon flinched at the cold touch of marble against his anus. He gasped as Brasius began to twist the phallus inside him. It pushed inside him, pressing against that spot that made him shiver with need, and his cock throbbed. He wanted desperately to be touched, and struggled not to beg for it.

"Thank you, Rennick," said Brasius, and the captain left them.

Brasius turned his attention back to Alysia. He stroked her breasts, pinched her nipples, and she began to moan, swinging in the harness.

"You have been well trained," he said to her. "I shall regret giving you up, but Jorell will treat you well."

Kynon gaped. *Jorell.* But Jorell was dead! Brasius's second in command had been dragged by his feet from the battlefield six months ago, an arrow in his chest and his guts spilling out of him.

Brasius caught Kynon's eye. "Yes, my princeling, Jorell. Your army celebrated prematurely on that count. He was sorely injured, and I promised him the prettiest girl in Caralis if he recovered. Today he will claim his prize."

Kynon didn't know what he'd expected, but the man who eventually arrived in the room didn't look like a monster. He was younger than the warlord. He had brown hair that gleamed red in the light. His face might have been handsome, except his nose had been broken several times in the past. His stormy blue eyes seemed clever, and his mouth curled into a smile as soon as he saw the tributes hanging in the harnesses. He walked forward, and Kynon saw his limp. He hoped Jorell would not repay Alysia for what the soldiers of Caralis had done to him.

"She's beautiful, my friend," Jorell said, standing in front of Alysia.

Brasius clapped him on the back. "And broken in nicely."

Alysia closed her eyes as her new master inspected her. When he reached out and cupped a scarred hand over her breast, she gasped and her eyes flashed open again. His other hand slipped between the lips of her cunt, and Kynon felt a sting of jealousy.

"Do you want a fuck, tribute?" Jorell asked Alysia with a knowing smile.

"Yes, master," she whispered.

Kynon watched through hooded eyes as Jorell unfastened his leggings. His cock was impressive and already hard. He took it in one hand and began to swing Alysia's harness with the other. He stood between her splayed legs, removed the phallus from her cunt, and timing the movement with the motion of the swinging harness, impaled her on his cock.

Alysia cried out. Unable to clasp her legs around him, she remained at his mercy as he used the sling to push her back and forth onto his cock.

Kynon didn't even realize Brasius had moved behind him until the warlord twisted the phallus free. Brasius swung him forward in the harness, holding him horizontally above the floor, facing the tiles. His master moved between his thighs with his cock ready.

Kynon swung in the harness like a

pendulum, his master's hands on his hips. Brasius's thick cock pushed into him, rode over that sensitive place deep inside, and then pulled out again. Kynon's weight forced him to take his master deeply every time. Each thrust was a new penetration, and Kynon began to tremble with the effort of not coming.

He looked over to Alysia and saw that Jorell was pounding into her now. She trembled in the harness, her golden hair almost sweeping the floor. She was writhing.

Brasius held the harness still suddenly, and Kynon came to rest against his master's cock. Unable to move any other way, he squeezed his muscles against it. Brasius pushed him away. He kept his cock inside Kynon now and began to thrust quickly.

Kynon caught Alysia's gaze and held it. Her face was flushed with desire, but her eyes conveyed more: *I'll miss you too.*

Kynon heard Alysia scream as she came, heard Jorell groaning as he came, and the sounds pushed him over the edge. His balls contracted, his cock released, and he came in spurts all over his abdomen and the floor. His spasming muscles milked his master's cock as well, and he felt the familiar blast of heat deep inside him.

Kynon felt a stab of despair as he realized he'd come without his master's permission. Another broken rule. He forgot his pleasure. His stomach churned as he twisted his head to look fearfully at the warlord. "I'm sorry, master!"

Even as he blurted out his anxious apology, Kynon castigated himself. His master hadn't asked a question. Why couldn't he just learn to shut his mouth? It wasn't difficult. It shouldn't have been, but gods, something about the way the warlord used him made Kynon forget his place.

Kynon knew instinctively that a punishment from the warlord would be worse than anything he had ever felt under Hera's dispassionate hand. The warlord was a monster. He braced himself for retribution that didn't come. Brasius only shook his head and ran his fingers along Kynon's lips gently. Kynon had expected a stinging punishment, and the tenderness startled him. He wanted to thank his master and had to clamp his lips shut to stop himself.

Brasius looked at Kynon a moment longer through narrowed eyes and then turned his back on him.

By Alysia, Jorell was gasping as he fastened his leggings again. "She's a beauty, Brase. Just beautiful."

"She has real fire in her," Brasius said. "You may even have the better deal of it, my friend."

It was like he'd been struck. Kynon struggled to keep his face impassive while his mind worked furiously. The casual observation hurt him more than a punishment would have, and he realized with horror it was because he *wanted* to please his master. It wasn't fair. The warlord had enslaved him, used him, and tormented him. He had forced Kynon to like it. The warlord had unmanned him completely. The casual comment was too cruel on top of everything else.

Too cruel for the warlord? he thought, biting his lip. No such thing.

Alysia threw him a sympathetic look.

Jorell didn't even glance at Kynon. It was apparent that Alysia delighted him. Even once he'd fucked her he couldn't keep his hands off her. He pinched her nipples and squeezed her breasts. "What's your name, tribute?"

"Alysia, master," she said, trembling under his hands.

"That's a beautiful name, Alysia," Jorell told her and leaned forward to kiss her on the lips. "You will call me Jorell."

Kynon's eyes widened. Jorell and not *master*? He glanced at Brasius in astonishment, wondering what his reaction would be to such a breach of etiquette, and discovered his master was looking back at him steadily. There was a questioning look in his eyes, as though Brasius was waiting for him to speak. Kynon's stomach clenched. He still felt the sting of his master's comment, and he remembered his training.

He quickly lowered his eyes.

*****

It hurt to lose Alysia. Kynon felt her absence

acutely. He hoped she would be happy with Jorell, or at least whatever passed for happiness in the unfamiliar vaulted halls of the citadel. He hoped, he supposed, that she would not be treated to any unnecessary indignities. Maybe that amounted to the same thing.

He slept fitfully that night, curled up on the mat at the foot of the large bed. He missed the sound of Alysia's breathing, the companionable, sympathetic silence of her presence, or their whispered conversations in the night when the warlord was sleeping. Kynon had never felt so alone.

Of all the things that had been taken from him since he was made a tribute, Kynon missed Alysia the most. He felt now how all the others must have: Arron, Breana, Renna, and all the rest. He was completely alone.

Guilt gnawed at his gut. He had been lucky to have Alysia by his side for so long. The others must have been even more terrified. They would have had nobody to whisper to in the dark about their fears, their shame, and their awful confusion.

"Do you like it?" Alysia had whispered to him once.

"I don't know." And Kynon had flushed immediately, thinking of his body's response to every new indignity. *"Do you?"*

"I do," she had murmured back, *"until I think about it."*

Kynon had been comforted to know that

because Alysia felt the same, he wasn't an abomination. He was sorry the other tributes had been denied that small consolation.

Kynon shifted, feeling the slender chain slither over his back. It was long enough to allow him some movement, but short enough that he could not get tangled in it. He had to be careful how he lay, turning his body to keep his collar close to the bedpost at all times. It was strange how his body had adjusted to the limitations of the chain. Even when he slept, he remained aware of the chain. He hadn't choked himself on it yet.

He could hear Brasius snoring gently.

"A guilty conscience," the philosopher Reiner had liked to say, *"will gnaw at your soul!"* In Reiner's world, there was order and balance. In Reiner's world, a warlord would hear the screams of the dead at night. His crimes would torment him.

Lucky for Brasius that he'd been raised with Segasa's relaxed code of morality, Kynon thought. If he'd been tutored by someone from Reiner's school of thought, he'd never sleep a wink.

Kynon sighed, shifting again. He wondered what Reiner would make of the monster who slept as soundly as a baby.

A sudden noise jolted Kynon upright. It sounded like a cannon. Kynon rose onto his knees, his heart thumping, and looked across to the window. He saw an explosion of brilliant green fire that lit up the sky, and gasped in astonishment.

The next explosion was red, and the one after

that was orange. Was it some form of artillery? Was it war? He shrank back against the foot of the bed.

Kynon didn't realize his master had woken until he felt his chain being released.

"Don't they have fireworks in Caralis, tribute?" Brasius asked through a yawn. "You needn't be afraid. Go on, go and have a look."

Kynon hurried to the window, leaning on the wide marble ledge and staring wide-eyed out over the city as it was showered in color. He cried out in astonishment and then clamped his hand over his mouth.

"My homecoming," Brasius said from behind him. He slipped his arms around Kynon's waist. "Lean back."

They watched the fireworks together.

Kynon frowned and bit his lip. He felt comfortable in his master's arms, but he didn't know what was expected of him. He remembered what Brasius had said to Jorell earlier that day in the training room: *You may even have the better deal of it.* Did this unexpected tender moment mean Brasius hadn't meant what he said, or was it another test?

He gasped as a shower of green blossomed in the sky.

Brasius's left hand found the scar on his hip and traced it. "Did you kill the man who did this?"

Kynon swallowed. He remembered very little about that terrible day. It was the first time he'd seen the warlord's army, and it had almost been the last. He had been sixteen, and he'd thought he was going to die. It had hurt so much he'd wanted to die. "I don't know, master."

"I hope you did," Brasius murmured in his ear.

Kynon swallowed again, twisting nervously. What did that mean? Gods, what did any of this mean? One minute he'd said Jorell had the better deal of it, and the next he was wishing Kynon had killed one of his own men in battle.

Red flares lit up the sky.

Brasius slipped his hand down to Kynon's cock and gripped it gently. He rubbed his thumb against the head, and Kynon began to move his hips. He stilled them with difficulty.

"You make me want to fuck you," Brasius whispered, his mouth against his ear.

You make me want to be fucked. Kynon bit back the reply and clenched his hands into fists, desperately trying to remember the rules. It didn't matter that he wanted to speak; his master hadn't asked him a question. He was a tribute now. His obedience was the price of peace, and he had already made too many mistakes. Kynon tried to ignore the feel of his master's hot breath against his throat and watched the sky through half-closed eyes. He heard the *whoosh* of a rocket being sent up, and then there was a second of silence before it exploded into red cascades that illuminated the rooftops of the city.

He hoped Alysia could see the fireworks

from wherever she was.

Brasius lubricated his hand with Kynon's precum and gripped his straining cock more tightly. He began to flick his wrist, and Kynon gasped and fought not to move.

"Do you know what you did wrong today?" Brasius asked in a low voice, his teeth worrying Kynon's throat.

Kynon groaned, twisting under Brasius's grip. "I came, master, without permission!"

Brasius raked his teeth across Kynon's prickling flesh. "No! You apologized!"

Kynon gasped and fought to keep his hips still. He didn't understand. He was trying so hard, and nothing he did was right.

Brasius reached his free hand up and twisted one of Kynon's gold rings.

Kynon cried out, desperately trying not to come as the jolt of pain went straight to his cock. He squeezed his eyes shut and shook his head.

"What are you doing?" Brasius growled, working his hand faster.

"I'm sorry, master," Kynon groaned. His first instinct was always to apologize. He didn't know what the warlord wanted from him, and it was too unfair. How could Kynon know what these people wanted if they didn't tell him? They had bound him up in their little rules, and he *liked* the rules even when he struggled with them. He understood the rules. This, whatever this was, was new, and Kynon distrusted it. Did the warlord want him to fail?

Because he was going to. He was going to come without permission. Twice in one day. It was unforgivable. Kynon bit his lip and tried desperately to ignore the feel of his master's hand on his cock. He whimpered in despair.

"What are you doing?" Brasius growled again, and Kynon heard the anger in his voice. "I want you to come for me!"

Kynon almost wept with relief. He accepted the moment for the gift it was and jerked his hips quickly. He ground himself into the warlord's fist.

"Tell me what you feel, tribute," Brasius demanded.

Kynon could feel his master's cock pressing against his hip. He searched desperately for some slavish words to appease the warlord. "Feels good, master. Thank you, master," he gasped. He came just as the sky turned green, jerking and shuddering into Brasius's fist.

Brasius wiped his hand on Kynon's chest and pushed him away.

Kynon wanted to be sick. He had displeased his master despite his best efforts. He was suddenly cold in the night air. He turned to face the warlord, his heart thumping. Should he prostrate himself on the floor? Should he beg for forgiveness? Should he open his mouth at all? Kynon swallowed, his throat dry. "Please, master," he said in a voice hardly louder than a whisper.

"Please, what?" the warlord asked.

Kynon hugged his arms to his chest. "Please

tell me what to do!"

The warlord's eyes flashed, and Kynon flinched back instinctively.

"You are not all that I had hoped," Brasius told him at last. There was nothing in his face to indicate it was a lie. The warlord didn't look cruel. He looked tired. "Get back on your mat, tribute."

Kynon felt a stab of pain and lowered his head so that Brasius could not see his tears. He shuffled back to his mat and dropped to his knees. Brasius reattached his chain and climbed back into bed.

Kynon clamped his hands over his mouth as silent sobs shook his body. He was trying too hard to be a good tribute and to please his master with docile obedience as Hera had trained him to do, and he was failing. And he hated himself for wanting to please the warlord. What had happened to his pride? He should have been glad the warlord wasn't pleased. It should have been his secret, fierce consolation in this terrible place.

The fireworks illuminated the room for a little while longer, but Kynon no longer cared. He kept his eyes squeezed shut and his hands over his mouth, afraid his master would hear his sobs.

Chapter Seven: Submission

"You may stand," said Hera. She sounded almost breathless with exertion.

The session had started like all the others. He had gone to his knees, his hands clasped behind his neck. He had waited patiently for Mistress Hera to instruct him, trying not to look at the walls. There were no artistic frescoes in the training rooms. The plain white plaster walls were hung with floggers, restraints, plugs, and other things Kynon hadn't recognized. It had shocked him. He couldn't imagine there was any terrible instrument of pain and pleasure that had not yet been introduced to his flesh.

It had been a long session, a difficult session, and Kynon had begun so badly.

Hera's voice had been soft at first. *"Do you find the rules difficult to understand?"* She had raised her eyebrows at his denial. *"You seem to have some difficulty in following them."*

He had stammered out an apology. *"I'm sorry, mistress!"*

"That was not a question." The slap to his face

had stung. *"Are you a fool? Are you a simpleton?"* She had frowned. *"Then we will start from the beginning!"*

Each of the rules had been repeated until Kynon had lost count, and punctuated with the sting of the flogger.

"You will assume the position."

"You will not speak unless it is to answer a question."

"You will not come without permission."

"You will obey."

It had been excruciating. Something in the pattern of the strokes had bothered him. It hadn't taken him to that place as quickly as he liked: the place where the pain spread into pleasure. It had worried him. He'd been unable to relax into the rhythm. Something was different. Kynon had twisted his head once to look up at Hera, and she had looked back at him through narrowed eyes, her lips pursed. Kynon had felt a thrill of fear: Was she angry? Was calm, dispassionate Mistress Hera angry? And then, like the fool Hera thought he was, Kynon had tried to dodge the flogger.

"Tribute!" Hera had demanded in astonishment. *"Have you learned nothing?"*

It was his own fault—he'd seen a white flash of pain when he had cracked his head against the tiles—and he had forced himself back onto his knees while the tears ran down his face. Somehow he had summoned the last of his failing strength to remain still for the next blow. And after that, he'd realized he could stay on his knees. Gods, why was that a lesson he always had to relearn? Why did every time he knelt before Hera feel like the first time? He trusted her; he trusted that the pain led to pleasure, so why did he have to master his fear every single time? Why was it always such a battle? What was *wrong* with him?

It had taken a long time, but eventually Kynon had redeemed himself and turned Hera's censure into guarded praise. The flogger felt good again. Hera's hand was steady again. It felt right at last, and he'd hated himself for entertaining that moment of ridiculous fear and doubt. He trusted Hera to know what was right for him, to know what his body could take, to know what he *needed*. At the end Kynon had been caught between pain and pleasure, each building on the last until he couldn't differentiate. Then, at the moment he'd been most afraid of failure, Hera had leaned down to his ear. *"You are not Kynon. You are Caralis. Do you understand?"* It had given him the strength not to beg to be allowed to come.

And finally it was over.

"You may stand," Hera said again, gently this time.

Kynon obeyed slowly, searching her face cautiously for signs of displeasure. Nothing. He'd misread it. He *was* a fool. His muscles ached from having knelt so long, and it was a relief to be able to move. The sting in his back defused slowly. Warmth spread through him. He drew deep breaths, trying to slow his racing heart.

Hera inspected the marks on his back and came to stand in front of him. Her stern face softened with approval. "Good. You have done well, tribute."

Kynon swelled with pride at Hera's rarely given praise. His legs were still shaking.

Hera gave him a moment to find his balance again and then led him out of the training room and down the passageway. Kynon had expected to be returned directly to the warlord's apartment, but Hera led him to a set of doors that opened onto a balcony. The cool sea breeze soothed Kynon's flesh.

Across a wide expanse of ornamental gardens and pathways was a large domed building. The gleaming, twisting towers of the citadel dwarfed it, and it seemed, to Kynon's untrained eye, almost modest in comparison.

"The senate," Hera told him, following his gaze. Her clever eyes were amused. "Doesn't it impress you, tribute? We must have spoiled you. It is better than anything Caralis has to offer, yes?"

She was teasing him, and Kynon flushed. "Yes, mistress."

"It is over three hundred years old," Hera told him. "It is built on the remains of the palace of the *kings*." Like all Segasans, she couldn't hide her contempt for the word. She saw Kynon's trepidation and smiled. "The true power of Segasa is not in the citadel, tribute. It is in the senate. It is the senators who watch your progress. Did you know that?"

Kynon shook his head. His temple ached,

and he resisted the urge to rub it.

"We take tributes often," Hera told him, "but it is a long time since we have had a prince. Normally they are not as pretty as you." She laughed.

Kynon smiled and looked at his feet.

Hera leaned on the rail of the balcony. Her hair flew in the breeze. "The senators are very interested in your training. They ask for daily reports. I will be pleased to tell them you did well today. It will go some way to making up for your previous failings."

Kynon looked worriedly at the senate building.

Hera touched him gently on the arm. "We have not discussed what happened on your first night here. Do you remember?"

"Do you mean when my master refused the senator?" Kynon asked warily.

Hera nodded. "It was not your fault. I understand that. The warlord is a stubborn man, but it was unseemly the way you clung to him. Do you see that?"

"I was afraid, mistress," Kynon said.

"But it showed disrespect to the senator," Hera said. "Again, it was not your fault. You were a prince, and I know this has been difficult for you. But you shame me when you forget your place, and you shame your country. It does not make the senate well disposed to Caralis when you are disobedient. You won't make such a mistake again, will you?"

"No, mistress," Kynon said anxiously.

"The warlord is your master, but he is not a procurator," Hera said. "He doesn't always know what is best for you. I know and the senate knows, so your training will continue despite your master's wishes. Do you understand?"

"Yes, mistress," Kynon said, his stomach twisting. He hoped the senate would not punish him for his master's arrogance, but trusted Hera to protect him.

"Good." Hera smiled again. "I am pleased, tribute."

She led him back inside.

*****

Brasius growled. "Enough!"

Kynon glanced anxiously at his master's face as the warlord inspected the marks on his body.

"Enough!"

Rennick reached for Kynon's face and turned it toward him. His gray-green eyes fixed on the bruise on his temple, and he shook his head slightly.

Brasius was angry. His hands were clenched into fists, and his neck was corded. His eyes, usually so dark, blazed. His handsome face was contorted with rage, and he was terrifying. It wasn't directed at Kynon, but it still scared him.

Kynon wished his master had heard Hera's gentle praise on the balcony instead of only seeing the mark of his failure.

"Enough," Brasius muttered. He reached out to touch Kynon and stopped himself as Kynon flinched away instinctively.

Rennick inspected the bruise. "An accident, perhaps?" His voice was doubtful.

"Tell me what happened," Brasius demanded.

Kynon flushed with shame.

"Tell me!"

Kynon met his master's eyes warily. "I fell. I was on my knees, and I tried to dodge the flogger. It was my fault, master." He should have known better than to try to move. It wasn't his first day anymore. *"Tribute! Have you learned nothing?"* Hera's rebuke had been as painful as his fall.

I did better at the end, master, he wanted to say. *I did better!* But he was too afraid of the anger written on his master's face to say it.

"I'm done with this," Brasius said, shaking his head.

Kynon dropped his eyes quickly, biting his lip in worry.

"The senate won't like it," Rennick said.

"The senate can fuck itself," Brasius said. "The tribute will have dinner at my side tonight."

Kynon exhaled slowly. Not done with him, then, not yet. He didn't know if the thought comforted him or not.

"Yes, sir," Rennick said to the warlord's back as Brasius slammed the door shut.

Kynon looked at the door anxiously as Rennick continued his inspection.

"You must be a slow learner, tribute," Rennick said. "Lie on your mat."

Kynon obeyed, stretching out on his stomach, and Rennick knelt beside him. Kynon closed his eyes as Rennick began to massage cool lotion onto his stinging back. His strong hands worked over each muscle, sometimes turning to dig his knuckles into the knots he found there.

"It's an honor that your master wants you at dinner," Rennick said.

Kynon sighed, flexing his aching shoulders.

Rennick continued to massage him. "There are other rewards as well, if you please him. When you're on your own, you can bathe if you want, or read books from your master's study."

Kynon twisted his head to look up, wide-eyed.

"You can read, can't you?" Rennick asked him curiously.

"I was tutored by a philosopher," Kynon said with a frown. "I'm not a *peasant*."

"Ah," said Rennick. "Now that's a word you might not want to use around here."

"Why not?" Kynon asked.

Rennick worked on his lower back. "People who talk about peasants, tribute, and in that tone of voice, are usually nobles. And we don't like nobles in Segasa."

"I don't understand," Kynon said. "My

master is a nobleman."

"He earned that," Rennick said in an easy voice. "The senate made him that. He wasn't some brat born to it." He smiled as Kynon flinched at the word *brat*. "We did away with all of that a long time ago."

"Did away with it?"

Rennick pressed his knuckles into Kynon's aching spine. "You ought to take note of the frescoes on the walls when you get the chance, tribute. And there will be a few books on the subject in your master's study."

The massage felt good after the flogging. Kynon remembered how Hera had held the flogger against his lips when she was finished and how he had thanked her and kissed the instrument of his torture. Even now he couldn't comprehend the thrill that had gone through him when he'd tasted the leather.

"This place must seem very strange to you," Rennick said. "But it will get easier. It might not seem like it now, from where you are, but we honor tributes."

Kynon couldn't stop a small, disbelieving snort.

Rennick laughed. "I know. You have to learn to trust the process, tribute. Things will look very different from the other side. You can believe that wholeheartedly."

"I'll try," Kynon murmured. He yawned, and his aching body slowly relaxed under Rennick's strong hands.

*****

Kynon, blindfolded, sat at his master's feet. His hands were chained behind his back. He could hear noise all around them, and he smelled hot food. Occasionally his master shifted in his seat and Kynon felt the touch of his hand against his lips as a morsel was passed down to him. Sometimes there was no food, only the intrusion of his master's fingers into his mouth. Kynon suckled obediently on those fingers. He shifted, his erection making him uncomfortable, and listened to the conversations taking place at the dining table instead.

The people at the table talked about things Kynon had long ago forgotten: wars and strategies and politics. Once upon a time he would have strained to catch every detail, but now he let the conversation drift above him like smoke.

"Jaran has sent a complaint," someone said, and Kynon started with surprise to hear his father's name. "He says to offer the serfs freehold will undermine the authority of the crown. He's not happy."

"I don't care," Brasius said. He inserted his finger into Kynon's mouth. "I've got all I want from him for now."

"We're all aware of that," said an amused voice. Was it Animon?

Someone laughed, and Kynon flushed with shame and pride at the same time.

Kynon was pulled up by his collar and drawn into Brasius's lap. He could feel his master's hard cock pressing against his thighs. He sighed as Brasius fed lazily on his mouth for a while, his tongue probing between Kynon's lips.

Brasius curled his hand around Kynon's cock. "We ought to turn our attention to Lutrica and hit them before the winter."

"We're not yet at full strength," Animon replied. "And you've just risked our senatorial support."

"They don't know that in Lutrica," Brasius said. "And the senate will come around. It always does." He rubbed his thumb over the head of Kynon's cock, and Kynon jerked his hips forward. Brasius laughed and pushed him gently back to the floor.

"Huh," said Animon. "Maybe you should have told the senate to fuck itself *before* you handed them the treasury of Caralis. We can't raise an army on an empty purse."

Kynon inhaled sharply and then frowned. No, this wasn't because of a tiny bruise on his tribute's temple. There were other things at play, political undercurrents that Kynon knew he didn't understand. He was a tribute. He didn't count for anything here. He rested his head against his master's thigh and inhaled his scent. He longed for more and hated that he did. He couldn't tell if the desire he felt was his own or if the procurators had trained it into him, and maybe it didn't matter. He only knew he wanted to insinuate himself between his master's thighs, to find his cock with his mouth and to suck it. Waiting was torture.

For the rest of the dinner Kynon concentrated on counting the seconds into minutes and the minutes into hours. Anything to keep his mind off his master's cock, or his own. He heard the clatter of dishes as the servants cleared the table, and then something else was brought out. Chess, he thought, listening to the scrape of the pieces being moved around and the snatches of conversation.

"Excellent move, sir!"

"You've left your rook open."

"You forget to play your queen early, Brasius! It is a costly mistake."

"Ha! That's a game you owe me!"

Kynon felt a longing for home. He had played chess before, in that half-forgotten previous life. He had whiled away many winter nights with games and conversations. He had been a person then. People had asked his thoughts, his opinions, and had listened to them even if they didn't agree with them. Now he was nothing.

"Lucky you plan your battle strategies better than your chess strategies, my lord!"

Kynon heard his master laugh loudly, and he almost smiled himself at the teasing insult. There was a time he would have thought Brasius the Warlord wouldn't hesitate to kill a man for saying such a thing, but he knew now that Brasius was generous with his friends. Kynon felt it was something he could have admired about the warlord, if he weren't his tribute. It was a strange contradiction that a man so good to his friends could otherwise be so cruel.

His master exhaled slowly, pondering some move on the board, Kynon supposed. It wasn't until he spoke that Kynon realized the conversation had shifted again. "The issue of freehold is not negotiable."

"It's Jaran's sticking point," one of the others answered.

Kynon frowned again. Of course it was. The king and the noblemen of Caralis owned the land. They had been born to rule it. His father was still the king, whether a client king or not. Kynon had paid the price to safeguard the crown of Caralis, as had every other tribute. The warlord had no right to change the terms of the deal now.

"Then he must be made to see the error of his thinking," Brasius said.

Kynon shivered. Somehow he had forgotten Brasius was more than his master. He was also his enemy. Kynon bowed his head and bit his lip. His face burned.

"And Lutrica?" Animon asked.

"Send an ambassador," Brasius said. "Offer them the usual terms and give them a month to respond. That way we can strike before winter if necessary."

What would happen to him, Kynon wondered, if Brasius went on a campaign? Kynon had forgotten how to live without a master. The thought made him sick, and he pushed it away. He was tired of living like this. He was tired of struggling between being a tribute and being himself. He was tired of not knowing which one he wanted to be. Sometimes he couldn't even tell the difference, he was so tired and the lines were so blurred. Gods, what more did these people want from him?

They had stopped giving him the procurators' blend. He no longer needed it to respond to his master's touch, but he wanted it back. It had dulled his mind. It had stopped him from asking himself too many difficult questions. Sometimes it had even stopped him from hating himself. Kynon remembered what he had told his master the morning they had entered the city: *I'm scared I'll lose myself more.* And it had happened. He wondered how long it would be until Brasius had destroyed him completely.

The evening wore on.

Kynon heard each of his master's dinner companions excuse themselves one by one, but Brasius seemed to be in no hurry to leave the table. He slid his hands down Kynon's back, found his shackled wrists, and unfastened the metal cuffs. Kynon's hands fell to his sides.

Brasius then reached forward and pulled Kynon's blindfold off. Kynon blinked in the light.

"Up," said Brasius, and Kynon climbed awkwardly to his feet.

The servants had cleared the large table. Nothing remained on it now but a jug of wine, his master's cup, and the chessboard. The dining room glimmered in the light of the chandeliers.

Kynon hugged his arms to his chest.

"Stand up straight, boy," said Brasius, looking him up and down. "Take some pride in yourself."

Kynon couldn't help the look of surprise that crossed over his face. *Pride?*

The warlord's lips curled into a slight smile. He nodded at the chessboard. "Do you play?"

"Yes, master," Kynon said.

Brasius hooked his boot around a footstool under the table and drew it out. He placed the chessboard on it and reached behind himself to retrieve a cushion. He tossed it onto the floor. "Sit."

Kynon obeyed, watching the board as Brasius began to place the pieces.

"You were listening tonight, yes?" the warlord asked.

"Yes, master," Kynon said.

Brasius looked down at him with raised brows. "And what is your opinion on what you overheard, tribute?"

Kynon dared to meet his eyes and hoped he was still talking about chess. The last thing he wanted was to talk about his father. "Animon the Destroyer of Cities is right, master. The queen is wasted defensively. The queen ought to be used to attack, early and often."

"Risk the queen too soon and risk the game," the warlord said. "Isn't that so?"

"Leave her doing nothing, and you might as well not play, master," Kynon replied hesitantly.

Brasius laughed. "Perhaps. Tell me, tribute, what is your forfeit?"

Kynon didn't know the term. "Forfeit?"

The warlord looked at him intently through his dark eyes. "I assume it is the custom even in Caralis to place a bet on the game. If you lose, what is your forfeit?"

Kynon's cheeks burned. He looked down.

"*Hmm.*" Brasius leaned back in his chair. "I'm sure I'll think of something."

Kynon felt a flash of anger at the teasing tone. He looked up again. "I do not doubt your ingenuity, *master*, but you may find you have already taken everything from me!"

"Everything?" Brasius asked, his mouth curling in amusement.

Kynon clenched his fists and dug his nails into his palms. Why did he always allow himself to feel those things he no longer had any right to feel: anger, humiliation, and shame? A tribute had no more right to those things than a piece of furniture. And why did Brasius always manage to goad him into them? Kynon wished desperately that those negative emotions were the worst feelings the warlord inspired in him but even now, wondering at the implications of a forfeit, his cock hardened.

Brasius laughed again. "Come, tribute, let us play."

Kynon controlled his breathing with difficulty and looked up again. He nodded.

Brasius moved his first pawn toward the middle of the board.

Kynon's hand trembled as he lifted his own pawn and pushed it forward hesitantly.

Brasius smiled slightly at his nerves.

Kynon's mind whirled. He had been good at chess. He was better than anyone back at the keep in Caralis. He was better than his father, better than his brothers, and better even than old Reiner who had taught him all the tricks of the game.

To be playing chess with the warlord Brasius! The man, enemy or not, was a genius when it came to strategy. In another life the chance to play chess with the warlord would have intrigued Kynon. Contests of physical ability and intelligence were common between rivals, a way to test the other's strengths and weaknesses. Kynon imagined an audience might have watched them at one time, playing ostensibly for amusement, but actually for so much more.

Except this was no chivalrous contest. Brasius was clothed, seated in a chair, and Kynon had to look up at him from his place on the floor, naked. Like a supplicant or a slave. Kynon flushed with shame. He had recalled, for one startling moment, the person he used to be. It was the prince's hands that felt the familiar weight and shape of the chess pieces, not the tribute's. The memory of the past few weeks threatened to overwhelm him, and he struggled to remember to breathe.

"An awkward juxtaposition," Brasius said quietly.

Kynon looked up at him warily.

"Your old life," Brasius said, "colliding with your new. It must be very discomforting."

"Yes, master," he managed.

Kynon played badly, too nervous, too conscious of Brasius's proximity. His master's hand brushed against his once, and Kynon almost jumped out of his skin. It made no sense. There was nothing the warlord had not done to him. A game of chess should not have been so humiliating. He thought it was the way the warlord now demanded his mind as well as his body. Kynon struggled with it. He resented Brasius more now than he had on that first night back in Caralis.

Brasius captured his queen. He leaned forward. "I've just thought of a forfeit for you, tribute. Put your hand on your cock."

Kynon obeyed. His cock leaped under his touch, jutting up toward his stomach. Brasius watched him through hooded eyes. "Now make your move."

Kynon pushed a rook forward.

"That was a mistake," Brasius told him in a low, amused voice. "Stroke yourself."

Kynon tightened his grip on his cock. He ran his hand from the base to the head, trying not to push his hips forward.

"Stop," Brasius said. He shifted in his seat, and Kynon could see the outline of his hard cock through his leggings. "Are you playing to lose, tribute?"

"No, master." Kynon flushed at the teasing tone.

Brasius captured his rook with a slight smile. "Do you always play so badly, or do you just want to touch yourself?"

Kynon bit his lip, embarrassed. "No, master. Um, I will try to play better."

"You will," Brasius said. "Stroke yourself again. Mind that you do not come."

Kynon obeyed, closing his eyes. His cock throbbed, and his balls had drawn tight. He recognized the signs and forced himself to think of something else to stop himself from coming.

The pattern of the tiles in the training room. A green and black geometric border, each section linking into the next. He knew it backward after this morning; it was what he had stared at when Hera flogged him, teased his cock, and tried to force him to come without permission. Kynon squeezed his eyes shut as his cock leaped in his fist. Green and black tiles. Green and black tiles.

"Stop," Brasius said, his voice low.

Kynon dropped his hand from his cock gratefully, his chest heaving with effort.

"You are were a noble-born prince," the warlord said, "a leader among men, and now you're stroking your cock in front of your enemy. What would your father say about that?"

Kynon stared up at the warlord through wide eyes. He tasted bile. Tears welled in his eyes.

A servant entered the room, unconcerned with the lewd display. She crossed the floor and placed a jug of wine on the table. "Commander, Lindus and his tribute are outside."

"Send them in," Brasius said. "This one can't play chess anyway. On your knees, tribute."

Lindus, Kynon thought, trying to keep his mind off what had just happened. A cavalry commander. Young for the position. Not a great military tactician, but a fearless commander. He led from the front. Kynon struggled to remember who the man's tribute was. Was it Breana?

"You missed dinner, my friend," Brasius said.

"I was introducing my tribute to my wife." The man laughed.

Kynon glanced up and felt a jolt of surprise. Lindus's tribute was *Arron*. He was naked, like Kynon, and his hands were bound behind his back. He had a single nipple ring through his left nipple. A green jewel hung from the ring, glinting in the candlelight. His cock looked as tormented as Kynon's, erect and straining against his stomach.

Kynon discovered he couldn't take his eyes off it.

Lindus was all angles. He was tall, thin, and sharp-eyed. He unbound Arron's wrists, patted him on the flank, and pushed him toward where Kynon was kneeling. "Kneel by the other tribute."

Arron obeyed, hanging his head.

Kynon could feel the heat of his friend's body and shifted uncomfortably.

"Drink?" Brasius poured Lindus a glass of wine.

"Thank you, Brasius." Lindus sat, stretching out his legs and resting his boots on an empty seat. "Tribute, you may play."

Kynon jolted in shock as Arron bent toward him, and then Arron's warm lips were pressing against his collarbone. Kynon looked up at Brasius, waiting for his master to prevent this as he'd prevented the senator from touching him on the first night in Segasa. He felt a rush of panic as the warlord regarded him with a smile. He had intended for this to happen, Kynon realized, even when he'd told Kynon to take some pride in himself. Even when they'd played chess. It was a fresh cruelty, and Kynon didn't understand it. It was his own fault. He should have known better than to remember he was a prince. He was nothing.

"I'm sorry." Arron whispered it so quietly that Kynon hardly heard him. He flicked his tongue against Kynon's skin.

Kynon looked up desperately at his master's amused face. It was his old life and his new one clashing again. It was why he was so horrified and why his master was so amused. He couldn't deny Arron's lips against his throat felt good. He couldn't deny his cock was already starting to leak precum. But he couldn't forget Arron had stood beside him as they faced the warlord's army and that they had sworn a brotherhood that was now being so defiled.

And it made the warlord's smile grow. "You are both free to come."

Kynon had loved Arron once as a friend and comrade, as a brother. It was like Conal all over again, except this time they were both being debased by the act. He tried not to feel it as Arron's hot mouth moved against his flesh.

"And does your wife enjoy him?" Brasius asked Lindus.

"What's not to enjoy?" Lindus laughed. "He plays so well with others. Yours?"

"He will learn," Brasius replied.

Kynon squirmed as Arron's mouth found his jaw, and tried to push him gently away. Arron's breath was warm against his ear as he whispered, "I'm sorry. Let it happen."

"Oh gods," Kynon whispered back. Arron slipped his hands around behind his back, and pressed his fingers into the tender welts on Kynon's skin. Kynon jerked forward, and then their cocks were touching.

Kynon thought of their fathers. One the king and the other the king's trusted steward. If they could see their sons now… This was wrong.

Arron shifted. He moved his mouth down

again, and Kynon's breath caught in his throat as Arron's lips fastened over his right nipple and his tongue flicked at the gold ring that pierced the tender flesh. His nipple hardened, and his cock throbbed.

"Gods." He closed his eyes and moved his hands through Arron's hair.

Arron reached a hand down between their sweaty bodies, pushing their cocks together and holding them. Kynon jerked his hips. He leaned his head back, exposing his throat again to Arron's mouth.

Arron kissed him under his jaw, and Kynon turned his head. He could feel his heartbeat thumping in his cock, he was so close to coming. He wanted to touch and to taste. He nuzzled his face against Arron's throat and licked his skin. It was warm and salty with sweat. He shivered.

Kynon was vaguely aware of Brasius and Lindus talking. Their voices were low and amused as they watched their tributes entangled together on the floor.

Arron groaned. His cock twitched, pressed against Kynon's, and Kynon shivered at the sensation. Arron still held their cocks pressed against each another, and Kynon began to rock his hips. Arron tightened his grip in response.

Kynon kissed him. Arron's lips and tongue were feverishly hot as they pressed into his own. Kynon could taste him. Kynon slipped an arm around his shoulder, pulling him closer. His free hand sought out the green jewel hanging from Arron's nipple ring, and he tugged it.

"Now," Arron whispered. "Together."

Arron gasped, grunted, and squeezed his hand tight around their slippery cocks. Kynon could feel their cocks spasming as they pushed their bodies against each another. They came together, cum spurting over each other's stomachs.

Kynon remembered what Arron had said on that hill above the town when the warlord's siege engines appeared on the horizon: *"Highness, are you ready to die?"*

And Kynon had smiled at him. *"We go as free men, together."*

Kynon gasped for breath. He pulled away from Arron, suddenly cold.

Arron turned away as well.

"Ah," said Lindus, "the afterglow of shame. Must be catching, eh? It's never bothered my tribute too much before."

Kynon sensed Arron squirm uncomfortably beside him and wished he could shut his ears.

"Mine blows hot and cold," Brasius agreed. He rose from his chair and moved around behind them. The warlord trailed his cool hand down Kynon's sweaty back, and Kynon shivered at the touch.

"Hands behind your back, tribute," Brasius said.

The cuffs were fastened again. Kynon closed his eyes as he was blindfolded, glad of the darkness.

On his knees, he listened as Brasius and Lindus played chess. They spoke in low voices that Kynon couldn't catch. He forced himself to relax instead, listening to Arron breathing beside him. He wondered how strange it would have felt if, instead of turning away from each other in shame, they had eked out the last of their bodily pleasure with soft words and gentle touches.

Then he hated himself for even imagining it. They weren't lovers; they were tributes. They had performed for their masters' amusement, like trained animals. He burned with shame.

It was late when his master led him back to his apartment.

"You're upset," Brasius said when he removed the blindfold. He reached down and gripped Kynon's cock, bringing it back to tumescence in a few easy strokes.

Kynon remembered his training and bowed his head. I hate you, he thought fiercely. I want you. He felt betrayed as well, and it made no sense. Just because his master had never beaten him didn't mean the warlord cared for his welfare. Kynon had mistaken apathy for affection. He was like a whipped dog, full of slavish devotion for the first man who fed him scraps without booting him in the ribs. No, he was lower than a dog. He was a *thing*, and he had no right to feel.

Brasius stroked his cheek, and Kynon had to force himself not to bend toward his touch. He accepted it passively instead, concentrating on controlling his breathing. Pleasure, just like pain, was not his to demand. It was his master's to bestow.

You are not the hostage here, he told himself. Caralis is the hostage.

He thought of his parents, of his brothers, and of all the people he had known back in Caralis. He could not fail them by being careless and undisciplined. Kynon hated to think what form of revenge the senate would take on Caralis if he could not correct his behavior. He heard Mistress Hera's voice in his head.

"You will assume the position."

"You will not speak unless it is to answer a question."

"You will not come without permission."

"You will obey."

Kynon opened his lips to accept his master's kiss. His heart beat faster as his master's tongue found his. It pressed, withdrew, pressed again. Kynon longed to crush his mouth to his master's, to push back, to lose himself in the kiss, but he was afraid. Tears pricked his eyes.

Brasius gripped his chin and angled his face upward. "Why are you crying, tribute?"

Kynon shook his head.

Brasius frowned. "*Talk!*"

Kynon felt a sob wrench out of him. "Because I don't know why you made that happen with Arron! Because I never know what you want from me!"

He expected punishment or stony silence and was surprised when the warlord's arms encircled him. He buried his face in his master's throat.

Brasius drew him to the bed, sitting back and taking Kynon with him. Kynon lay with his back against his master's chest. His tears made him feel more exposed, and he wanted to curl up. His master's hands, linked together across his stomach, prevented it.

"Do you know why I let the ambassador's son take you that time?" The warlord's fingers traced the path of the scar on Kynon's hip gently.

Kynon, remembering the humiliation, shook his head and struggled to control his tears.

"Do you know why I asked you to play chess tonight?" Brasius rubbed his cheek against Kynon's ear, and Kynon felt the scratch of stubble. "Why I chose Lindus's tribute to play with you? I do these things to draw out my enemies. Because the prince of Caralis is my enemy, and the soldier of Caralis is my enemy. I want to rid you of them."

"Impossible," Kynon murmured.

"No," said Brasius. "Not impossible at all. Strip them away and the boy remains. And his tears will dry in time."

Kynon shook his head. "But I have tried to be a good tribute, master!"

Brasius snorted. "Tributes! If I wanted to fuck a sack of potatoes, I'd fetch one from the kitchens! I want your fire. Do you understand that? You had it when you were on the blend. I know it's still there."

Kynon closed his eyes. "Then give me the blend again, master."

Brasius tightened his grip, and Kynon could feel his master's hard cock pressing against the small of his back. "No. I want all of you."

Kynon's heart skipped a beat. Brasius's voice was so low, so intense that he didn't know what to say.

"And I want you to give it to me." Brasius slipped his hand lower and stroked Kynon's cock lightly for a moment.

"I don't understand," Kynon whispered, biting his lip.

"You can, and you will," said Brasius, moving his hand back to Kynon's stomach. "Do you trust me, boy?"

Kynon was afraid that the answer, wrenched from deep inside him, made him a traitor to Caralis and to everything he was. "Yes, master!"

Brasius hummed in pleasure against his throat, and Kynon shivered as the sound vibrated against his flesh. "Good boy."

Brasius shifted, depositing Kynon on the bed beside him. The mattress felt impossibly soft after all those nights spent on the floor, and Kynon sank into it wonderingly.

"You will sleep here tonight," Brasius said.

"Yes, master," Kynon said and allowed himself to slip easily into Brasius's embrace. One of Brasius's hands lay against his hip. The other had found his collar, and Brasius hooked his fingers through it gently. Kynon, wrestling with his wild thoughts, expected it would take him a long time to fall asleep. He hadn't counted on the way his tears had wrung him out, on the softness of the mattress, or on his master's astonishing tenderness. He couldn't struggle anymore, not against his master, not against his past, and not even against sleep. He drifted off listening to the sound of his master's deep breaths.

Chapter Eight: Correction

From the window in the warlord's bedroom Kynon could look out over the colorful, beautiful city and see the gray ocean. Kynon sometimes passed the hours by counting the trading ships he saw and marveling at Segasa's wealth. It was a vibrant city, and a part of Kynon longed to explore the twisting streets outside the citadel. In the beginning he had imagined finding his way to the port and hiding aboard one of those exotic trading ships. He had liked to think of the strange lands they could carry him to, if he weren't a tribute.

More often than not Brasius had already left by the time Kynon awoke. To the senate, or the city, or whatever it was the warlord did when he was not at war. Nobody had ever bothered to explain it to Kynon.

Shortly after dawn Captain Rennick would arrive, and Kynon would be taken to the bathroom, where he would be thoroughly cleaned — he no longer felt any indignity at the captain's invasive methods — and then buffed gently with pumice. Then Rennick would shave him, carefully working the razor over his jaw and then to his underarms, chest, and abdomen. Kynon didn't even get scared anymore when Rennick worked the razor close to his cock and balls. After the shave, he was buffed again until his skin was soft and sensitive, and then lotion was rubbed in. Rennick would massage him, working out all the knots and aches from the day before and from the night spent sleeping on the floor. He would eat a meal of bread, meat, fruit, and water, and then Rennick would take him down to training with Hera.

The long afternoons without Brasius felt like they lasted years. Kynon was grateful for the books in the study.

Kynon, looking down from the windows of his master's study, saw into a garden on a private terrace. He knew the garden was private because he had never seen anyone in it, and because it was full of the most striking flowers he had ever seen. Even from several floors up their colors were vibrant. If it had been a public terrace, Kynon imagined it would have swarmed with people.

Kynon often stood at the window of his master's study and looked down at the garden. He wished he could feel the sunlight on his back. He hated the long afternoons and needed all the distraction he could find. He missed his training sessions. He missed his master. He missed Alysia. He was lonely.

Kynon was about to turn away from the window when he saw Brasius walk onto the terrace.

He would know him anywhere. There was a dog gamboling around his legs and a little girl on his back. Kynon was shocked. He had never seen Brasius so carefree, so open. He wouldn't have imagined it was possible if he hadn't seen it himself.

Rennick found him standing by the window in his master's study and peered outside. "Fen," he told him. "Brasius's daughter."

"I didn't know he had a daughter," Kynon said, surprised. He had seen Brasius as a friend and now as a father, and a part of him knew it would have been easier if Brasius were still just a monster in his mind, the terrible, fearsome warlord. Seeing him like that, swinging his daughter around in the garden, made Kynon feel more alone. He would never know that man.

"That's because your father's spies are rubbish," Rennick said.

Kynon didn't respond.

"That was a joke, tribute," Rennick said. "Come on. Let's get you loosened up."

They returned to the bedroom, and Kynon lay on his mat as Rennick worked over his muscles.

"Have you seen Alysia?" he asked.

"She is well," Rennick said. "Her master is very pleased with her, Procurator Loran is very pleased with her, and she is glowing. Jorell doesn't leave her side."

Kynon was almost jealous.

"Come on, now," Rennick said. "Time for a session."

Kynon looked at him in surprise. "But it's the afternoon, and I'm not due any correction!"

Rennick helped him to his feet. "This session is by special order of the senate." He squeezed Kynon's shoulder to reassure him. "Don't be afraid. Your master has arranged it. He will be there with you, and it will be good, tribute, if you let it."

*****

Kynon had expected Hera would be waiting for him in the training room, but instead he saw a man in a blue procurator's robe and Brasius. Kynon felt a rush of anxiety. He looked to his master for reassurance, but it wasn't Brasius who spoke.

The earnest-faced young man looked him in the eye. "Commander Brasius has asked the senate to administer this test today, against the recommendation of the mistress procurator. The senate has acquiesced."

Test? Kynon's breath caught in his throat. Against Hera's recommendation? He was afraid.

The man's voice was calm. "I am Procurator Loran. You will not disappoint me, will you?"

Kynon recognized the name. Loran was Alysia's trainer. He looked at the man curiously. He was thin and pale. His unremarkable face seemed kind.

"No, master," Kynon said hesitantly. It was strange to call another man that.

The procurator nodded. "Well, we will see."

The room was not Hera's. Kynon's eyes widened as he looked around. The place looked like a cross between an engineer's workshop and a stable. There were trestles and crossbeams and benches all around the room, and whips and bits and shackles hanging from the wall.

Loran clasped his hands behind his back and looked him up and down. "Have you been stretched today?"

Kynon looked at the floor, flushing. "No, master."

"Then we will start with that," Loran said.

He led him to a padded bench in the middle of the room. Kynon lay over it, taking his weight on his stomach awkwardly. His ankles and wrists were shackled, stretching his body into a taut bow. He felt Loran's cool hands spread his buttocks, and he began to gently twist an oiled plug into his anus. It was quite narrow at the beginning and easy to accommodate. It felt like a series of rings. It grew wider at the base, and Kynon felt sweat break out on his body as he struggled to accept it. At last his muscles closed over the bulbous end. Kynon panted with the effort. It was wider than a cock at the base and deeper. He was afraid it would do him some injury. He looked fearfully at Brasius, and the warlord stared back at him. The look on his face was impossible to read.

Loran massaged his lower back. "Relax, tribute."

The ache in his lower back began to fade, but

the plug was so large, so uncomfortable that Kynon tried to move restlessly against the restraints. He could feel the seams on the leather plug rubbing against his inner muscles.

After some time, Loran released him. He told Kynon to stand, and he tried to obey. The sting of pain in his anus from the plug as he shifted position made him cry out and try to expel it.

"Stand," Loran repeated quietly.

He groaned, struggling to obey.

"Why aren't you hard?" Loran asked him.

"It hurts, master," Kynon managed. His body was still trying to bear down. He couldn't do this. This was worse than anything Hera had prepared him for, and she'd known it. It wasn't Hera who had put him here when he wasn't ready, when he didn't deserve it. It was Brasius.

Loran shook his head at him and produced a leather harness from the wall. "I'll have to strap it in place if you can't be trusted to hold it there."

"Careful, Loran!" Brasius growled, and Kynon turned his eyes toward him beseechingly.

"Master, please!" he gasped.

"It is the standard test, Commander," Loran said calmly. "Please try to remember you are here to observe only. That is the compromise the senate has allowed. I will not harm him, I promise. I will remind you that the mistress procurator cautioned the senate about your tribute's inexperience."

Brasius's face was set.

Kynon cried out as Loran pushed on the plug

with the heel of his hand, driving it back inside him. The procurator threaded the harness through his thighs and around his waist. He cinched it, forcing the plug deeper inside him. Kynon almost screamed.

"Relax," Loran said sternly. He reached down and held Kynon's flaccid cock in his palm. He closed his fingers around it. "Relax."

Kynon closed his eyes as Loran began to tug gently on his cock. He tried to ignore the pain and concentrate on the pleasure. His balls tightened, and his cock stiffened at last. Loran gripped the base of his cock, preventing his release, and Kynon drew in a sharp breath that hurt deep in his guts.

"Your master will ring your cock if he wishes to keep you stiff without coming," Loran told him. "I will demonstrate."

Kynon flinched as a hard ring snapped around the base of his cock where Loran's fingers had been. His cock, pointing up toward his stomach, throbbed, but with the blood flow restricted, he could not come. Kynon had never known anything like the awful, wonderful sensation it produced.

Loran reached up and twisted the rings in his nipples, and his whole body jerked. His cock was painfully hard.

"A ring can keep you hard for days," Loran told him, and Kynon shuddered at the terrible thought.

Loran shackled his wrists behind his back.

"On your knees," he said, helping him to the floor.

Loran attached a spreader bar between his knees, forcing his legs apart. He placed a blindfold over Kynon's eyes and then forced something into his mouth. The ball filled his mouth entirely, pressing his tongue down. It was attached to straps that Loran bound behind Kynon's head. Then Loran pushed his shoulders down toward the floor.

Kynon couldn't see. The ball made it difficult to breathe, and the plug in his ass and the ring around his cock tormented him. He couldn't move, and so he knelt there, his forehead pressed against the floor and his ass in the air.

"He is struggling, Commander," Loran said.

"He can do it," Brasius replied. "He'll pass."

The procurator sounded less sure. "He is not ready for this, Commander."

Kynon knelt there and waited, and nothing happened. He didn't even know if Loran and Brasius were still in the room. He tried to count the minutes, but his mind was drowned out by the needs of his throbbing, shivering body. His skin pricked, and his sweat was cold. The muscles in his thighs ached, but any attempt to modify his position shifted the plug deep inside him, and he trembled with pain even while his hard cock throbbed.

His breathing grew fast. He was overcome with sensation. His throat was dry and he couldn't swallow, but he could feel spittle on his chin, leaking out from behind the ball gag. He couldn't see anything, and he had lost track of the time. He turned his head back and forth, trying to catch any sounds. Anticipation made him want to cry.

He desperately wanted to come. He was held on the edge, held immobile, and his entire body shuddered in need. He knew without a doubt that he would have come, over and over, if his cock hadn't been ringed.

The day drew on, the exquisite torment with it, and at last Kynon began to cry. The procurator must have been watching from somewhere, because as soon as he saw Kynon's body heave with sobs, Loran was by his side. The feel of his cool hand down his spine made Kynon arch and moan.

Loran removed the gag. He stroked his face, and Kynon blindly tried to kiss his hands. Next Loran released his knees and helped him to his feet. Panting with exertion and with desire, Kynon allowed himself to be walked blindfolded back to Brasius's apartment and left on his knees in the bathroom.

Was it over? He didn't know. He cried again as he waited.

*****

Kynon, caught in a tortured dream, didn't even know anyone was there until he felt his left nipple ring twisted. He cried out and arched his back, pushing blindly toward the pain.

"Master, please," he groaned, unable to stop

himself. "Please fuck me."

He heard Brasius's low chuckle and turned his face toward the sound. Fingers gripped his jaw, and a ball gag was inserted into his mouth. Kynon groaned around it as it was fastened behind his head.

His master moved around behind him, and Kynon presented himself as he'd been bound in the training room: knees spread wide, ass up, and his forehead on the floor. He felt his master's fingers on his hips, fiddling with the straps of the harness. It fell free at last, and then Brasius began to remove the plug. Kynon groaned into the gag as each segment of the plug pushed against the sensitive place inside him.

Then the warm head of Brasius's cock was pressing against his opening. His master pushed inside him with no preamble. The leather plug had done its work well. He slid in smoothly, quickly, and deeply. Kynon clenched his muscles gratefully around his master's thick cock. He squeezed, and his master's cock twitched inside him.

Brasius began to fuck him. It was hard and fast, and Kynon pushed back to meet each thrust. His master gripped him by the collar, forcing him to keep his head down, and with his other hand raked his fingers down Kynon's spine. Kynon tried to arch his back, couldn't, and moaned. His cock was hard and had been hard for hours now with no promise of release. It was torture.

Brasius pulled him up by the collar, crushing

his bound arms between them. Kynon felt his master's mouth on his neck, and then his teeth, and he tensed as Brasius bit him on the muscle between his neck and his shoulder. Kynon jerked as he felt his master's teeth break his skin. The white flash of pain went straight to his balls.

"Come for me, boy," Brasius commanded, and Kynon shook his head and tried to talk through the gag. He felt blood trickling down his torso.

Brasius pulled him almost upright with one hand and reached around them both with his other hand, searching for Kynon's engorged cock. Kynon heard him laugh as he found the forgotten ring. Brasius fumbled with it for a moment, and then the clasp gave out.

Kynon's balls contracted as Brasius gripped his cock, and his cock swelled. He screamed behind the gag and came over his master's hand.

Brasius released his collar, and Kynon dropped panting to the tiles. The warlord unbound his hands and rolled Kynon carefully onto his back. Brasius unfastened the gag and removed it from Kynon's aching jaw and then pulled off the blindfold.

It was night.

Brasius moved from the floor into the sunken bath and beckoned Kynon to join him. His muscles aching, his shoulder stinging, Kynon obeyed. The hot water soothed him.

Brasius leaned against the back of the bath. "Come here."

Kynon moved over toward him, and Brasius pulled him onto his lap and drew him into a warm embrace. He lay back against his master's broad chest, turning his face toward his throat, and sighed when he felt Brasius's cock rubbing against the small of his back.

Brasius folded his arms around Kynon. "You did well today, boy. You were worth the wait."

Kynon swelled with pride. He ran his lips along Brasius's jaw, all the pain and frustration of his session forgotten. "So were you, master." He sighed. "Did I pass the test, master?"

Brasius ran his hand ran along the muscles of his abdomen. "It's not my decision, tribute. You were good though. You were better than good."

Kynon shivered with pleasure and tilted his hips to feel Brasius's cock rub against the cleft of his buttocks.

"Insatiable little slut," murmured Brasius, smiling. He curled his fingers around Kynon's cock. "Mount me."

Kynon shifted, feeling Brasius's cockhead notch against his anus. He rose in the water and eased himself down. He shivered as he felt his master's cock push into him, inch by inch. Brasius let him set the slow rhythm, leaning his head back as Kynon began to ride him gently.

"Tell me you want it," Brasius groaned.

"I want it," Kynon managed. "I want you to fuck me, master."

"Work for it!"

Kynon closed his eyes and concentrated on squeezing his master's cock. He loved to have Brasius inside him. It felt good. It felt right. He loved to make this man come, and he loved it when Brasius allowed him the same pleasure.

Brasius gripped Kynon's cock more tightly as Kynon began to move.

"Did it hurt you today?" Brasius growled.

"Hurt like hell," Kynon said, and he felt Brasius's cock leap inside him. He arched his back. "Wanted you so bad, master."

"Did you like it?" Brasius pulled his head back by the collar and licked the place he'd bitten.

"Loved it, master," Kynon gasped, riding him faster. "Master!"

He came, feeling Brasius come at the same time. Hot and fast and deep inside him. Kynon slipped off him and then turned back and nestled into his embrace. Brasius toyed with the rings in his nipples, and Kynon pressed his lips to his master's throat and kissed him.

Later, after he had taken a towel and rubbed down his master's wet body, Kynon knelt obediently on the rug at the end of the bed. His master ran his hands through Kynon's damp hair. He smiled as Kynon leaned into the touch. He did not chain him.

"Good boy," he said and crawled into his bed. "You've found your fire again."

Kynon, tired and aching, and sated for the first time in days, was already dozing when he heard his master's voice.

"Tribute?"

"Yes, master?" he responded in a drowsy murmur.

"Come and lie with me."

Kynon's heart beat faster as he lay down on the bed, facing his master. He felt Brasius's hand slide over his hip. His cock hardened almost immediately, pressing against Brasius's abdomen.

Brasius smiled, his eyes half-closed. "I'm tired, tribute. Keep that thing to yourself."

Kynon tried not to smile at his tone. "I'm sorry, master," he murmured.

"Roll over," Brasius said.

Kynon obeyed. He was surprised and gratified when Brasius pulled him closer. He nestled into the warlord's embrace. Brasius flung an arm over his hip, his hand coming to rest gently on his cock.

Kynon sighed as his master stroked him tenderly several times and then moved his hand away. He shifted uncomfortably, his erection growing.

"Get some sleep, tribute," Brasius said into his ear.

Kynon sighed again and closed his eyes. It occurred to him as he drifted off that nobody had even told him why he was being tested, and he knew it wasn't his place to ask.

******

Kynon awoke from an unsettling dream. His hands went to his throat, checking that his collar was still in place. It comforted him, he realized. Like a dumb animal content to know its place, or a happy slave. Normally the realization would have made him sick to his stomach, but tonight Kynon didn't feel it. Too much had changed for that.

He lay on his back in Brasius's bed. Brasius was sleeping on his stomach, one arm stretched over Kynon's abdomen. Kynon looked at the planes of the warlord's body, hidden in shadow and moonlight.

If your father could see you now, the voice in his mind said, but Kynon didn't let it finish. He can't see me, he told the voice. He won't see me. It was liberating.

It had rained. Kynon smelled it in the air.

He slipped from underneath Brasius's arm and climbed to his knees above his master. He reached out tentatively and brushed his fingers against Brasius's hip. Brasius sighed in his sleep.

Kynon's throat was dry. He'd never touched his master without invitation, and it felt strange to do it now. He traced his hand toward Brasius's spine, feeling the muscles in his back.

"I should hate you," he whispered, frowning. "Why don't I hate you?" He felt the warmth that radiated from his master's body, and he shivered. He leaned down and pressed his lips against Brasius's spine, tasting salt and sweat and heat.

Brasius shifted underneath him, and Kynon froze. He heard his master sigh again and relaxed. He thought his master was still asleep and almost jumped out of his skin when Brasius spoke. "You don't hate me, because you trust me to know what feels right for you."

Brasius rolled over onto his back, and Kynon moved away anxiously.

"No," said his master. "Follow your instincts."

Kynon met his master's eyes in the darkness and reached out a trembling hand to feel his chest. "Like that?"

Brasius smiled slightly. "Like you want, tribute."

Kynon forced himself to relax, counting his breaths. He could feel his master's heartbeat under his fingers. His exploration became more confident. He ran a palm over Brasius's nipple, and it hardened under his touch. He heard Brasius's sharp intake of breath and smiled. He had made the warlord gasp with nothing more than the gentle pressure of his touch. His chest swelled with pride.

"Feels good, doesn't it?" Brasius murmured. "To have another man in your control?"

Kynon snorted. "You're not in my control, master!"

"Try me," Brasius murmured.

Kynon gazed down at his master with wide eyes. He wondered if he had the courage to order his master to lie still or to move into a different position. He shivered at the thought and shook his head. "No, master, I can't do that."

Brasius didn't push him. He caught Kynon's hand and brought it to his mouth. He nipped at his fingertips. "Do you know the most empowering thing about having another human being submit to you?"

Kynon shook his head.

Brasius smiled and released his hand. "The trust. It's not about pain or power or even about coming. It's about trust. I know how difficult it has been for you. I know how much I have tested you, but you trust me now, don't you?"

"Yes, master," Kynon said without hesitation. Every indignity he had suffered had led to greater pleasure in the end. The pain and the humiliation were worth it.

"And what have you learned?" Brasius asked him. He reached out for Kynon's hand again and drew it down to his hardening cock.

Kynon closed his fingers around the warm shaft of flesh. "Learned?"

"What have you learned about yourself?" Brasius asked, shifting his hips as Kynon began to stroke him.

Kynon frowned as he worked his master's cock. "I'm not sure. I don't recognize myself, if that's what you mean."

Brasius laughed quietly. "That's a start."

Kynon smiled at the sound of the warlord's laugh. He bent and flicked his tongue against the thick head of Brasius's cock. The shaft swelled in his grasp, and the warlord sighed pleasurably.

"Mount me," Brasius said.

Kynon straddled him, and Brasius gripped his hips tightly. Kynon reached down and angled his master's cock underneath him, pressed it against his burning hole. He sank down with a gasp. His muscles stretched and fluttered around Brasius's cock, and he groaned.

"Don't move," Brasius said, holding him still.

Kynon bit his lip and nodded. The muscles in his thighs ached. Brasius's cock was massive inside him, almost too painful. He needed friction to transform the sensation into pleasure. Sweat trickled down his temples. Every muscle, every nerve in his body screamed at him to move. He moaned.

"I wish you could see how beautiful you look," Brasius sighed. "When you struggle, you're exquisite."

"Master," Kynon groaned. He arched his back to try and relieve the pressure.

"*Shh,*" Brasius said. "Don't move."

Kynon squeezed his eyes shut.

"To make a man submit," Brasius said, "you first have to know yourself. The limits of your own cruelty, of your own passions. Your own tolerance for pain. You have to learn to read a man. One day, tribute, you'll see the look on a man's face as he fights himself to obey you."

Kynon counted his breaths.

"To master another man, you first have to master yourself," Brasius said. "You need to know this."

Kynon shook his head. "Tribute. Just a tribute."

Brasius exhaled slowly. "I don't want just a tribute. You know what I want."

Kynon clenched and unclenched his jaw. He nodded, almost sobbing with pain and desire. "Me. You want all of me."

"Good boy," Brasius said. He angled his hips and thrust.

Kynon cried out in relief as his master's cock pushed into him. "Thank you, master!"

Brasius gripped his hips again and held him, and Kynon moaned in disappointment. The warlord's voice was low. "And do you know the worst thing about having a man submit to you?"

Kynon bit his lip and shook his head. "No, master!"

Brasius's voice was strained. "You have to know when to stop!"

Kynon's eyes flashed open. "Please, no, master. Don't stop now!"

Brasius laughed, digging his fingers into Kynon's flesh tightly. Kynon felt the warlord's cock twitch inside him. "Don't move. Don't move."

Kynon dropped his chin to his chest, desperately trying to obey. He was helpless, impaled, and he couldn't stop trembling. His cock was hard, pressed up against his stomach, and his balls were tight. He knew he'd come the second Brasius thrust again. He concentrated on his breathing, but he was wound too tightly to relax.

Brasius released one of his hands, trusting him not to move. He raised his hand to Kynon's face. "You're doing so well," he said.

Kynon turned his face to catch his master's fingers in his mouth. He frowned. "Are you training me now, master?"

Brasius smiled. "In my own way, tribute."

Kynon moaned. "Please, master. Please let me move."

"What would you do if I didn't?" Brasius asked him in a low voice, withdrawing his hand.

Kynon tried not to rock his hips just thinking about it. He bit his lip. "I'm on top. I'd move anyway!"

Brasius groaned, laughed, and tugged at the ring in his left nipple. "Follow your instincts, boy. Give me all of you."

"Master!" Kynon arched his back, feeling Brasius's cock swell inside him. He raised himself up with his knees and then impaled himself again onto Brasius's cock. He managed one stroke and then another before he came wildly over his master's stomach and chest. At the same moment Brasius lifted his hips from the bed and thrust into him deeply. His master's cock swelled again, squeezed by Kynon's spasming muscles, and Kynon cried out as he felt the blast of heat deep inside his body.

"No more training," Brasius murmured. "No more procurators, no more senators. You're mine, all mine."

"The test?" Kynon asked breathlessly, and Brasius smiled.

He fell forward into his master's embrace, and Brasius kissed his hair, his forehead, his lips, and his throat. Kynon, his body aching, lay contentedly in master's sweaty embrace and sighed under his kisses.

*****

Kynon, drifting slowly off to sleep, didn't hear the door open at first. Brasius's cock was pressed against the cleft in his buttocks, flaccid but still large, and he didn't want to move. His master's arms were around him, pulling him back against his chest. He had one hand curled around under the collar at Kynon's throat, and the other one lay on his sticky cock. Kynon could feel Brasius's breath against his ear. He didn't know Mistress Hera had even entered the room until she was standing right above them in the brilliant moonlight.

She looked down at them, and her face twisted.

Kynon saw the transformation a fraction too late. He closed his eyes, feigning sleep. He hoped that she hadn't seen he was awake.

He kept his eyes squeezed shut for a long time.

Kynon's heart beat faster, and Brasius tightened his arms around him in his sleep as he trembled. It felt safe.

When he opened his eyes again, Hera was gone.

Chapter Nine: Punishment

Kynon awoke to find the sunlight streaming through the bedroom window. He stretched and realized he was still lying in his master's bed. The mattress was thick and comfortable, and the bedding, which smelled of his master, was soft. Kynon luxuriated for a moment in the warmth of the bed, turning his face to the pillow to catch his master's scent. Brasius had already left, and Kynon wondered what it would be like to wake up with his master's arms around him.

He found that his head was still spinning from the night before. Brasius had been pleased with him, but it was more than that. Brasius didn't want a tribute—a sack of potatoes—he wanted Kynon, and last night he'd finally got him. *"I want all of you,"* he had said, and Kynon felt his chest swell at the memory. He wished his master didn't have to speak in the senate today. Something about Lutrica, he had said sometime before dawn. Kynon didn't remember—he had been so astonished to find himself having a conversation with the warlord that didn't involve fucking that his brain hadn't taken much in. Something about Lutrica and whether they would agree to the treaty, and how Segasa would respond if they didn't. Kynon didn't care. He wasn't a prince anymore, and he wasn't a soldier. Brasius had done what he'd promised, and rid Kynon of them. He was just the boy now, and the boy liked — *loved?* — his master.

No. He turned his face into the pillow. Liked. That was all. That was enough. That was too much, probably. Gods, what was wrong with him?

He rose at last and went to the bathroom to wash. The water in the sunken bath, not drained since the day before, was cool. Kynon washed slowly, using the sponge to remind his flesh of the torment and pleasure of the day before. He ached, but his body was sated. He reached up to the collar around his neck.

He climbed out of the bath and dried himself.

One of the servants had left food on the desk in the study: fruit, bread, and water. Kynon sat on the floor by the desk, eating his breakfast and flicking through the pages of a book of poetry. He was unsurprised to discover it was bellicose stuff. He closed the book and reached for another one. It was a history of Segasa.

Kynon realized he would be more comfortable if he sat in the chair, but he had never been able to bring himself to do it. He thought he might take the book back to Brasius's bed and read it there.

Kynon heard the door to the apartment open.

He closed the book and slipped it onto the desk, hoping it was Brasius. His breath quickened, his balls tightened, and his skin prickled. He wondered what wonderful torment Brasius had dreamed up for him now, what new lesson he had to teach his tribute, and his heart beat faster.

Hera walked into the room. Kynon began climbing to his knees before he even realized what he was doing, and then fought the instinct and sat back. *"No more procurators, no more senators,"* Brasius had said, and Kynon believed it. The warlord had never lied to him, not even at his most cruel.

Hera sat in the chair by the desk and looked out the window for a while. She said nothing.

Kynon rose to his feet without being commanded and regarded her carefully. He counted his breaths and willed himself into calm stillness.

Hera turned back to face him again at last. Her voice was mild. "How quickly you have forgotten the rules."

Kynon saw her gaze settle on the small wounds between his shoulder and his throat where Brasius had bitten him.

"Was your master pleased?" she asked.

Kynon folded his arms across his chest. "Yes. It pleases my master that I have finished my training."

Hera raised her eyebrows at his show of defiance. "You master is neither a procurator nor a senator, tribute. Perhaps you ought to remember that."

Kynon stared back at her. "What do you mean?"

"Commander Brasius does not train the tributes," Hera said, her voice cold. "The procurators train the tributes. It is my honor and my privilege to do so. The warlord is not the ultimate authority in Segasa, whatever you might think. It is the senate that really holds your chains. Do you remember the night you arrived here? Do you remember the offense that Commander Brasius gave to the senator?"

Kynon nodded.

Hera smiled slightly. "And then there was yesterday. For three hundred years the senate has charged the procurators to train our tributes. For three hundred years we have been able to do so without interference. Do you know what happened yesterday? Do you know that the warlord demanded the senate administer the test before you were ready?"

"I do," Kynon said. His stomach was in knots. His bravado flooded away under the force of her cool stare, and he added, hesitantly, "Mistress."

Hera's face softened at the word. "Then you must realize the senate will support me when I tell them you failed, tribute."

Failed? But his master had said he'd done well. What mistakes had he made? What else could he have done? Kynon felt bile rise in his throat. "But why, mistress? I obeyed!"

"I did not ask for your response," Hera said quietly, shaking her head. "You cannot remember even the simplest of rules, and you have to ask why! You can't hold your tongue, much less your composure. The warlord is your master, tribute, but I am the mistress procurator. I am responsible for *all* of the tributes. If you cannot remember your training, and if Commander Brasius will not correct you for your mistakes, I will have the senate assign you to another master. I could have you chained in another bedchamber by the day's end."

Kynon flinched.

"I warned him you were not ready." Hera sighed. "But of course it is confusing to you. I understand that your master is more to blame than you are. Perhaps another master would serve all our interests better."

Kynon fought against a rush of panic. Because of Caralis, he assured himself. Because the warlord had chosen him, and it was only right that he served the warlord. But he knew it was a lie. He didn't just crave Brasius physically anymore. It had gone beyond that. He hoped she wouldn't see the tears pricking his eyes as the realization hit him. "I can't," he said, his voice faltering. "Mistress, you mean I can't be what he wants me to be."

Her face seemed sympathetic. There were dark shadows under her eyes that morning, and her voice sounded kind. "Your master makes things difficult, yes? And you want to stay with him?"

Kynon nodded.

"If that is the truth," Hera said, "you will prove it. Assume the position."

Kynon went anxiously to his knees and clasped his hands behind his neck. He had no doubt Hera had the power to take him from Brasius. And he couldn't lose him now, just when he'd begun to reconcile the monster and the man in his mind.

He watched as Hera ran her fingers down the cover of the book he had been reading. Kynon had hardly got past the first few pages. He had wanted to learn why there were no kings in Segasa. He hadn't yet discovered how and why Segasa had, as Rennick had put it, done away with all that.

Reiner had told Kynon that kings and princes were born to rule. It was the natural order. It was the will of the gods. Kynon had never questioned it. He wondered why the people of Segasa once had. And why they still believed it so strongly that their conquered kings were told to give the serfs ownership of the lands they worked.

Reiner had also told him the people of Segasa were morally corrupt. And yet Segasa was beautiful.

Hera sighed and crossed her ankles. "Perhaps you were not ready to be taken off the blend. Did you like the blend, tribute?"

"Yes, mistress," he said, flushing. "The blend made me eager, but now you and the senate don't want me to be eager."

Hera smiled. "You are too clever, tribute. That is your difficulty. The blend is indeed used to make a new tribute eager, but eagerness is not obedience. Do you know why we take tributes off the blend once they are here?"

"No, mistress."

"Because we want them to remember they have already begged to be taken in every way and that there is no point in refusing now. They no longer need it." She smiled again. "The blend lowers your resistance, but it is the flogger and the shame that teach obedience. Do you understand?"

"I want all of you," Brasius had said. *"And I want you to give it to me."* His heart beat faster remembering the hunger in his master's voice.

Kynon stared at the floor. "I'm sorry, mistress. Am I not to want to be used?"

"You may want it all you like," said Hera. "But it is not your place to demand it."

Kynon remembered how he had pushed back against Brasius in the bath the night before. How he had later explored the warlord's body with his hands. It had felt good. It had felt right.

"You are a tribute," Hera said. "Your will, your desires, your thoughts — they are meaningless. That is what you are here to learn."

Kynon opened his mouth and closed it again.

Hera's eyes danced with amusement. "You may speak."

"Thank you, mistress," he said. It frightened him how easy it was to sink back into obedience. "For what purpose am I here to learn those things?"

Hera raised her eyebrows. "I do not believe a

tribute has ever asked me that question. No, it does not displease me. You are not here to learn it for your benefit, tribute, or even our benefit. You are here to learn it on behalf of your people. You are here to demonstrate to them the power of Segasa, so that they wish never to have to learn it for themselves."

Kynon nodded, and remembered that he was not Brasius's tribute. He belonged to all of Segasa. And he was not Kynon. He was Caralis.

Hera opened the book and flicked through the pages. She found the one she was looking for and showed him the illustration. Kynon saw a woman wearing a gold collar. She had wide hips, skin the color of milk, and large breasts. Her nipples were ringed, just like his own.

"This is a tribute," Hera said, "but not as you understand them. This was a common peasant. In the time of kings, at every harvest feast, a woman was given to the king. And he married her and made her a queen, and then, at the next harvest feast, he sacrificed her to the gods by burning her alive."

Kynon's mouth dropped open.

"And so Segasa rid herself of her kings," said Hera. "And her gods. But the ideas of the tributes and sacrifice remained. We take them now from our enemies, and we are pleased to remember that we are not as cruel as those ancient kings, because our tributes are given freedom and honor at the end of their term instead of death."

Freedom, Kynon thought, and honor. The concepts had become so alien to him that he had no idea what to make of them.

"But you must earn them," said Hera. "Do you understand how?"

Kynon looked at the picture and thought of sacrifice. "By obedience, mistress."

She smiled at him. "Yes, by obedience. Come and stand here."

Kynon rose, the muscles in his thighs aching. Hera took him by the hips and positioned him against the desk. "Lie back. It is time for a lesson in obedience."

Kynon obeyed, embarrassed when she pushed his knees up and apart and he was completely exposed to her. His cock, which had lain dormant during their conversation, twitched to life. He felt as Alysia must have back in Caralis with Brasius standing between her legs.

Hera stroked the taut inside of his thigh, her fingers skirting close to his balls. "How large is your master's cock?"

"I don't know, mistress," Kynon said, trying not to tremble in response to her gentle touch.

"How many fingers?" she asked him, holding up her hand. "Or is it as thick as my wrist?"

Kynon's stomach clenched. Surely she didn't mean to do what he thought she did. He wet his lips with his tongue nervously. "Um, I don't know, mistress."

"I do, as it happens," Hera said. She slipped

her hand inside the folds of her robe and brought out a narrow flask. Kynon watched as she unstoppered it and dripped oil onto her fingers.

Kynon breathed deeply as her first finger circled his anus, pressing at the ring of muscle there. He felt the pressure of her fingernail against the sensitive flesh, and then the finger slipped inside him. It twisted, stroked, and Kynon bore down. It slipped in deeper and withdrew. Then he felt two fingers.

Kynon clamped his lips and frowned in worry.

She scissored her fingers inside him.

The third one hurt him, and he flinched.

He wanted to beg her to stop, but her eyes, fixed on his, were determined.

This has to be, he thought desperately. He remembered what Hera had whispered to him that day in training and clung to it now. *Mistress Hera is Segasa, and you are Caralis. This is symbolic. This is necessary.* He tried to believe it but couldn't. Not for those reasons. But it was still necessary.

Not for Caralis, Kynon realized, and not for Segasa. And certainly not for some bullshit symbolism that was so important to the senate, but for himself. If he wanted to stay with Brasius — and gods help him, he did — then this was necessary.

He bit his lip so hard when her fourth finger pressed into him that he drew blood. It hurt even more than the first time Brasius had fucked him, but he tried to embrace it. He groaned in despair as her thumb pressed against his aching entrance.

Kynon wished he were bound. It took all his self-control not to throw her off. She was a woman, smaller than him. He could easily do it, he knew, but he didn't dare. This was *necessary*.

"Has your master never done this?" she asked curiously.

Kynon opened his eyes. He could hardly see her through his tears. "No, mistress."

"Pity," she said and pushed forward.

Kynon cried out as her knuckles breached him. He gripped the sides of the desk, trying desperately not to kick out. The pain there was like nothing he had ever experienced. He wanted to scream.

He turned his head and saw the picture of the ancient tribute. Her face was pale and her eyes were large.

He felt as though he was being ripped apart as the widest part of Hera's hand pushed inextricably inside him. Even the pressure of her fingers against his gland didn't ease the pain. He felt wetness, too much for the oil, and wondered if he'd pissed himself. Then he realized it must have been blood.

And suddenly the defending muscles of his anus had closed over her wrist. He was almost glad of the pain then, almost. It kept him from imagining how he must have looked, how low, how degraded, and how despoiled.

"There now," Hera said. ""Are you still with

me, tribute?"

Through his tears, Kynon saw her eyes flash. He couldn't tell if it was with anger or with pleasure.

"It hurts," he managed. "Please, mistress, it hurts!"

"Calm yourself," she said, smiling tightly. "There is only a little blood. When I say, I want you to clench around me."

Tears streamed down Kynon's face. He cried out as he felt her hand move inside him and realized she was drawing her fingers into a fist. Pain tore through him. His entire body throbbed with it.

"You are doing very well," she told him. "Now, clench for me."

He bit back the yelp of pain that escaped him as he obeyed.

"Good," she said, relaxing her fingers. "We're almost there. Relax for me, and I will withdraw."

Kynon began to cry.

Hera drew back slowly. The widest part of her hand tore at the ring of his anus. It stung and burned, and then she was standing before him, wiping her hand on her robes.

"Do you know why I did that, tribute?" she asked.

Kynon shook his head, trying uselessly to bite back tears.

"Because you have forgotten your place. You do not sleep in your master's bed. You are not a lover. You are *nothing*." She looked down at him as though she were about to strike him, and then her face softened with a sympathetic smile. "Obedience is not always easy. You may put your legs down."

Kynon shifted and realized that the pain was still with him. He lowered his legs slowly, afraid to move too much. His body heaved with sobs.

Hera looked down at him dispassionately. "I will correct you further this afternoon. In the meantime you can think about how to improve your behavior. You may thank me."

"Thank you, mistress," Kynon said through his tears.

Her cold, noble face had never frightened him as much.

******

Afterward, moving awkwardly, Kynon took a bath. The water stung him, and he flinched when he lowered himself into it. He had brought the book with him and placed it on a folded towel on the floor above the sunken bath. He was careful not to get it wet. He hated to think what would happen to the intricate illustrations if they met water.

He rested his folded arms on the side of the pool, feeling the warmth soak through the tiles. He looked at the picture of the ancient tribute and wondered why the book hadn't named her. Had she even existed, or was the picture a composite of all the unfortunate women who had been sacrificed to the ancient Segasan kings?

The book was not new, but Kynon imagined he could still smell the cinnabar, verdigris, and saffron that had been bound as pigments to illuminate the illustrations. The colors were still vibrant. Like everything else in Segasa, the book was a thing of beauty.

Such a refined people, Kynon thought, with such a refined cruelty.

He closed his eyes, pushing away his disquiet with difficulty. He didn't understand why it was so hard to be obedient and passive. He would have preferred to be at the other end of the spectrum, fighting his subjugation all the way instead of wanting it. It was still disobedience, but Kynon felt it was a form of disobedience he would have understood.

Kynon didn't know what had happened to him. He had been utterly debased, transformed into something he couldn't recognize, but the process had been so alien, so confusing that he hadn't realized with each step he took that he was tangling himself further into their web. And whenever he thought he was close to understanding, it seemed as though the rules changed.

Kynon opened his eyes. No, the rules had never changed. Mistress Hera had made that perfectly clear. It didn't matter that Brasius had wanted him to break them. He was caught between Brasius and between Hera and the senate. Like a fly in a web while the spiders fought over him.

His life had been a good one. He had been born a prince. He had obeyed his father and his king. He had been dutiful to his mother and respectful to his brothers. He had been courteous to his tutors, except maybe old Reiner. He had been a good soldier. Not as great as Tolan or Nemic, but he had done his best. He had done everything that he had ever felt was expected of him, even down to asking Alysia Varne for a kiss behind the armory wall.

In all those years he could only think of one single time he'd been defiant enough to do the wrong thing: in the passageway of Hailon Castle, when he'd run bodily into the warlord. *"You're in my way."* It was the bravest, most stupid thing he'd ever done. And look where it had got him.

The second bravest thing? Banging on the door and demanding to see his father after being made a tribute back in Caralis. And look where it had got him.

Reiner had had a term for it: *hubris*.

His brother Tolan had had a phrase for it as well: *"That'll come back and bite you in the ass."* Tolan's seemed more apt.

His mistakes had brought him to Segasa, to the warlord Brasius, and to the frightening traditions of Hera and the faceless senate. His disobedience had well and truly bitten him in the ass. If he'd apologized in Hailon, if he'd been obedient since the beginning, if Brasius hadn't encouraged him to follow his instincts…

Disobedience only ever led to trouble. Now it threatened to take him away from the one thing he shouldn't even have wanted: Brasius.

Kynon groaned, resisting the urge to smack his head on the tiles until things started to make sense. Because he'd knock himself unconscious, slip into the bath, and drown before that happened.

He rose out of the bath after a while, careful not to drip water onto the book. He carried it back to the study wrapped in a towel, and placed it back on Brasius's desk. He dried himself with the towel.

"Tribute?" a voice called from the doorway of the apartment.

It was a procurator. Warily, Kynon walked out to meet the man.

"You will come with me," said the procurator. "Mistress Hera awaits you."

Kynon's throat swelled with tears, and he steeled himself against them.

The procurator looked at him curiously. "I didn't take you for trouble. No one's ever needed this much correction. What are you doing wrong?"

Kynon drew a deep breath and centered himself. He had to force himself to obey. He had to do this, to submit to Mistress Hera and the wishes of the senate, if he wanted to stay with his master. And even if he didn't know anything else, Kynon knew he wanted that. "I'll do better."

Kynon leaned his head forward to let the man hook a chain to his collar and allowed himself to be led placidly from the room.

*****

She was going to kill him.

"Farther," said Mistress Hera, and Kynon yelped behind the gag as the chains were tightened. This correction was his worst session yet. Mistress Hera had called him insolent, unworthy because he couldn't keep his cock hard without a ring while she caned him. Kynon wanted to please her, but he knew he was failing. Something had changed. Suddenly submission wasn't good enough.

He had tried to beg, but the gag prevented it. He had tried to beseech her with his eyes: *Why? Why are you hurting me?* but Hera's face was cold and proud and set like stone.

Kynon was suspended spread-eagled from chains. The cuffs bit into his wrists and ankles, and he felt sure he was about to be ripped apart.

The man turning the winch grunted with the effort.

"Now, whip him," said Hera.

It wasn't a flogger this time, but a proper whip with a single long, sharp tail.

Kynon tried to scream as the whip caught his back. He felt the stinging lash against his flesh. His flesh split, and blood coursed down his back. He tried to jerk away, and something in his shoulder tore—a new agony.

Tears ran down his face as his body burned.

"Keep going," Hera said.

The pain was worse than anything he had ever felt. Worse than in the stable yard back in Caralis. Worse than any time with the flogger. Worse than anything he had even imagined.

The whip caught his flesh again, cutting and gouging. His flesh was being flayed from his body. Kynon jerked uselessly. Blood ran down his legs and dripped off his heels. The room stank of it.

His mind clambered for an escape his body couldn't find, and the stench of his blood took him back to the battlefield. Mud and noise and smoke and blood. And he was lying there, thrashing, and Tolan was kneeling over him with his hands pressed against the gaping wound on his hip.

"Kill me," he'd begged. *"Make it stop."*

"It's not so bad, little brother," Tolan had told him. *"It's just a scratch!"* But his eyes had been dark with worry.

"Make it stop!"

"Don't fight it," Tolan had told him. *"Rise above it."*

"Can't!"

"You can," Tolan had told him fiercely. *"There's a place it doesn't hurt. Find it."*

That place, Kynon had thought later, was blood loss; when he was too weak to even moan, he'd drifted, his mind unanchored and beyond caring about his body. Later, much later, he'd been embarrassed about what he'd begged Tolan to do, but Tolan had never mentioned it to anyone else.

Could he find that place again without Tolan

by his side? Could he go there? Tears streamed down his face. Where was Tolan? Where was anyone? Where was Brasius?

The whip struck him again, and every nerve in his body screamed. He tried to beg, but the words caught behind the gag. The noises he made were animalistic grunts and moans, drowned out by the whistle of the whip and the wet cracks it made when it connected.

He tried to scream — nothing but a high-pitched whine.

"Keep going," Hera told the man.

"Mistress Procurator," he gasped, "he's had more than enough."

"How dare you tell me my business!" she said. "Get out. I'll do it myself!"

Kynon bucked against the chains as he heard the door slam. *Don't leave me with her!* he tried to beg, but the only noises he made were small and pathetic.

"You are nobody," Hera said. "You are *nothing*!"

Kynon wept, his chest heaving with the effort. She hated him, Kynon realized. She *hated* him, and he'd tried so hard to obey.

Hera raised the whip, and Kynon's entire body jerked as she brought it down. The tail struck his buttocks, one searing lash curling down across his anus, all the way through to his balls. He screamed through the gag, and his head lolled forward onto his chest as he slumped down.

"The warlord defies the senate, defies me, for *you*," she hissed. "Three centuries of tradition, and you are *nothing*!"

Kynon whimpered.

"Are you hard yet, tribute?" Hera asked in a cool voice, mocking him. She came to stand in front of him. "No?"

Kynon tried to plead with his eyes.

Hera raised the whip again and let the bloody tail run across her palm. "Lift your head, tribute."

Kynon only closed his eyes.

"Lift your head, you insolent mongrel, or I'll strike your eyes!"

Kynon, weeping, managed to obey. His head hung back, exposing his chest and throat to the procurator. He didn't even have the strength to brace himself for the blow.

"What the hell is this?" The voice was familiar, but Kynon, in his pain and his panic, couldn't place it.

"You have no right to intrude on a procurator's training!" Hera snapped.

"Like hell I don't!"

Kynon opened his eyes in time to see Captain Rennick wrench the whip from Hera's hand and cast it onto the floor.

"How dare you?" she snarled. "How dare you raise your hand to me?"

"Leave now, Procurator, before I dare it again," he returned, and she stormed away.

Kynon tried to speak and whimpered behind his gag.

"It's all right," said Rennick. He moved behind Kynon and began to unwinch the chains. Kynon sagged to the floor, and Rennick laid him down gently and unshackled him. He reached behind Kynon's head to unfasten the gag.

Horses. Rennick smelled of horses.

"It's all right," Rennick said as he eased the gag out of his mouth. "I'm here."

Kynon gasped for breath and started to cry.

Afterward, he couldn't remember too much. He had screamed when Rennick picked him up, but the rest was a blur of stairs and passages and horrified faces as the captain had carried him downstairs to his small room. He had been laid on his stomach on the captain's bed, and he remembered he had made a fuss about it as well, about getting blood everywhere.

"You let me worry about that," Rennick had said.

Afterward, there had been a doctor, or a succession of them, and whatever they had prescribed had sent him spiraling into wild dreams. He was being hunted and couldn't move, and then it had him and its teeth had torn his flesh. He woke up screaming and discovered it was night and that his back was on fire.

Alysia was kneeling beside the bed, her lovely eyes wide with worry. She was clothed, and Kynon's eyes widened at the strange sight.

"Why are you here?" he asked, and his voice cracked.

She stroked his hair, too afraid to touch him anywhere else. "Jorell thought you might need me here."

Kynon focused his eyes with difficulty. "Where is my master?"

Rennick rose from the stool he had been sitting on. "The senate."

Kynon felt tears well. "Will he come?"

Rennick gave him a sympathetic smile. "No, not just now. You need to sleep, tribute. You need to recover your strength. You need time."

Something was different. Kynon raised his hand to his naked throat, and he drew a shaky breath. "Where's my collar?"

"We had to take it off," Alysia said.

Kynon was tired. "Will he come?" he asked Alysia.

"*Shh,*" she said, stroking his hair. "Sleep now."

*****

In the darkness, Kynon heard voices intruding rudely on his dreams. Was that Rennick? Almost certainly that was Rennick, explaining in his calm and easy voice exactly what had happened.

"He wasn't in your apartment, so I went to check the training rooms. The assistant ran past me, pale as a ghost, so I went in. I found him suspended," Rennick said, "and blood everywhere. Well, you've seen the room."

"Yes, I've seen it." The voice was low and dangerous.

Was that his *master*? Kynon tried to open his eyes and couldn't. He was too tired.

"I should have been there," Rennick said, and this time Kynon heard a hard edge to the captain's voice. "Whatever happened, it wasn't training."

It wasn't your fault, Kynon wanted to say. *You were always good to me, Rennick.* His lips moved, but no sounds came out. He'd used them all up behind the gag in the training room, he supposed.

Rennick spoke again. "If word gets out that we treat our tributes like this, we won't get any more. They won't bow down even when they're beaten, if this is how it is."

"I know." Kynon heard Brasius sigh. "We'll make it right with Caralis."

"With Caralis?" Rennick asked him. "What about with *him*?"

I'm here, Kynon wanted to say. *I'm awake.* But he was already drifting again.

That same tired sigh again. "Keep him here. Fix him."

Kynon heard the sound of boots scuffing the floor.

"Sir?"

"What is it?" Brasius's voice came from somewhere different now. He was standing. Was he leaving? Kynon tried to speak again and couldn't.

"You might want to ask yourself why she did this," Rennick said. "What makes this tribute so different?"

Kynon heard the door slam. He sighed and drifted back toward the comforting oblivion of sleep.

Chapter Ten: Recovery

Kynon didn't know if it had been hours or days before he woke again. He was numb, unaware of any pain, but something warned him not to move and test it. He felt warm and bulky and realized he was wrapped in bandages. The bandages stank like rotting seaweed. Kynon didn't even have the strength to wrinkle his nose at the smell. He could barely keep his eyes open.

The room was small. There was no vaulted ceiling, no frescoes, and no intricate tiled patterns on the floor. The walls were plain plaster and unadorned. The bedding was rough.

There was a man sitting in the chair. Sunlight streamed through the small window behind him. It caught in Kynon's eyelashes and blinded him.

"Rennick?" Kynon asked. "What happened?"

"It's not Rennick," the man said.

Kynon recognized Brasius's voice and tried to rise. Pain ripped through his back, and he fell back onto his stomach.

"Don't move," Brasius said. He leaned forward, out of the blinding light, and Kynon saw his eyes were darker than usual. His forehead was creased with a frown, and his jaw was clenched tightly. He was angry.

"I'm sorry, master," Kynon said. He couldn't read the look that flashed across Brasius's face.

"What are you sorry for?"

"I failed," Kynon managed. Tears swelled in his throat. "The senate will take me away from you."

For a moment he thought Brasius was going to say something, and then suddenly the warlord stood. He stared down at Kynon, his face set like stone, and then turned and left the room.

Don't go, Kynon wanted to say, but it was already too late. He was alone.

*****

It was a long time before Rennick would let Kynon up from the bed for anything other than to use the chamber pot. Even that Rennick carried over to him so he didn't have to walk far. Rennick changed Kynon's dressings daily and massaged his muscles so that they didn't begin to waste away. He brought Kynon books as well, and food, and Kynon passed the days lying on his stomach and listening to the captain read to him in a voice that was both animated and educated.

"You don't just look after horses and tributes, do you?" Kynon asked him wryly one afternoon after Rennick had read him a lengthy poem without even faltering over the archaic words.

"I attended the university, if that's what you mean." Rennick smiled, knowing it was.

"And you became a soldier?"

"I do the work I like," Rennick said. "It doesn't mean I don't have a mind."

"I didn't mean any offense," Kynon said.

"I know." Rennick began to read the next poem, and Kynon closed his eyes to listen.

After a fortnight, the doctors pronounced Kynon well enough to move about, but not before he had to listen to a pair of them lecture him on what he could and couldn't expect his body to do. When they took his bandages off, Kynon asked for a mirror.

It hurt to twist and try and see his scars, but he forced himself to look. His back was like an angry web. The scars, still fresh and red, stood out in raised welts from his shoulders to his buttocks. Tears welled in Kynon's eyes as he looked at them.

"It's all right," Rennick told him. "You still have a lot of healing to do. They'll improve."

Kynon hoped he was right. He had never been vain, but the idea he would carry such ugly scars for the rest of his life mortified him. It meant he would never forget. Had Brasius only really valued his good looks? Were his scars the reason he hadn't stayed?

Rennick produced a pair of loose leggings and helped him dress. Kynon had been without clothes for so long that he felt awkward as he stepped into the leggings. His fingers fumbled as he tied the drawstring.

"There," Rennick said. "Now you're ready for an outing."

"An outing?" Kynon asked warily.

"A picnic," Rennick said and laughed at the look on his face.

Kynon turned as he heard the knock on the door. It opened, and he saw Alysia standing there.

"You're wearing clothes!" he said, astonished. "I thought I'd dreamed it!"

She smiled. "So are you."

Kynon was anxious to be leaving the sanctuary of Rennick's room. Alysia, sensing his discomfort, squeezed his hand tightly and drew him along.

The passages at the back of the citadel were narrow and dark, but gradually they opened into wider, sunlit spaces decorated with colorful frescoes. Kynon didn't know where Alysia was leading him as she drew him up a set of wide, sweeping steps, and he was surprised when she flung open a pair of doors and he found himself looking out into the terrace garden he had often watched from Brasius's window.

There was a large blanket lying on the swathe of soft grass near the fountain. Alysia drew him over to it and sat down beside him.

"You can lie down if you want," she told him, and stretching out under the sun, Kynon obeyed. He eased onto his back, listening to the gentle burble of the nearby fountain. He lay on the blanket, letting the sun warm his bare chest. The leggings felt odd. The touch of the fabric against his skin was strangely restrictive to him now.

The doctors had agreed that sunlight would help him heal. Alysia had been given strict instructions not to allow him too long on each side. The last thing he needed was to burn. Kynon was uneasy about turning his back to the sun. He was worried it would hurt.

Kynon opened his eyes as he heard uneven footsteps, one boot dragging on the path, and knew it was Jorell. He was unsure how to greet the man. Jorell saw his unease and waved it away. He set down a basket. He had brought a picnic.

Kynon hadn't fed himself for so long in company that at first he had been nervous about reaching over to help himself, and Alysia laughingly fed him his first slice of fruit. It was sweet and unfamiliar to him. He ate several pieces, but he wasn't hungry. He was content to just feel the sun on his skin and listen to the fountain.

Alysia, dressed in a flowing green gown, looked lovely. She looked lovelier than Kynon had ever known her. She was happy. She was sitting between Jorell's knees, leaning against his chest and holding his scarred arms around herself. Kynon couldn't see, but from the look on Jorell's face, he guessed the way Alysia had been playfully rubbing herself up against him had greatly affected him. He narrowed his eyes at every teasing look she threw him over her shoulder, like he wanted nothing more than to rip her clothes off and take her then and there. And only a few weeks ago, he might have. But something had changed between them. They were not master and tribute anymore. They reminded Kynon more of giggling newlyweds. They even talked of the same silly things that newlyweds did: furnishings.

"It's awful," said Alysia. "I won't have it in our bedroom!"

Won't. A word Kynon didn't remember.

"That couch was my grandfather's," Jorell protested. "It's an antique."

"It's an eyesore," Alysia said. "And it's moth-eaten."

"They don't make fabric like that anymore," Jorell said.

"Thank the gods," Alysia said, and he laughed.

They thought Kynon was asleep.

He felt his throat tighten as he listened to them. He was envious of Alysia, he realized. She'd been given to a man who obviously adored her, and Kynon had gotten Brasius. He'd thought they were something more than master and tribute as well, but where had Brasius been since Hera had whipped him? All that tenderness, all that exploration, and it was all bullshit.

Kynon tried not to cry. How often had he stood looking down into this garden? He wondered if, from that window several stories up, Brasius was watching him. Kynon inhaled deeply and shifted his arm, making a show of waking up. He peered up at what he thought was the right window, but couldn't tell if there was anyone there.

Alysia was at his side immediately. "You ought to turn over now, Kynon."

She helped him. Alysia had seen him before his wounds had healed into the angry scars he now wore across his back, and was unsurprised. Jorell had not. As Alysia helped him roll onto his stomach, Kynon heard Jorell murmur something in surprise under his breath. He flushed.

"You can only have a few minutes," Alysia told him.

"No," Kynon whispered. "I want to go back inside. Please take me back inside."

He couldn't bear Jorell's scrutiny.

It was Jorell who helped him up carefully, and Kynon was struck by the strangeness of it. Two enemies, both disfigured by the hatred and rage of each other's countrymen, and one helping the other find his feet in the quiet, sunlit garden.

"We've all got scars, tribute," Jorell told him quietly. He looked down at his arms and seemed to lose himself for a moment in memory. Alysia touched his arm, drawing him back into the present, and he smiled at her.

Alysia squeezed Jorell's hand.

Kynon felt it again, a jolt of surprizing, painful jealousy. He turned his face away to hide his misery.

*****

Kynon healed slowly. Thanks to the doctors in Segasa, he healed well. His scars would never disappear entirely, the somber doctors told him, but they would fade in time.

Doctors were not his only visitors. Rennick's humble room on the first floor of the citadel, with a single window that overlooked the massive stable yard, was suddenly on the map for more than a few important people. Senators came to visit, and procurators and viziers and magistrates. Kynon didn't like being the center of so much attention and was nervous and withdrawn, particularly with the procurators. One of them, Loran, came accompanied by Alysia.

"Loran trained me," Alysia said. Her blue eyes shone with devotion as she looked at the procurator. "He was good to me."

Kynon remembered Loran from his test but refused to be ashamed.

"What happened to you, tribute, was an anomaly," Loran said in an apologetic tone. "A good procurator explores the relationship between pleasure and pain, between Dominant and submissive, between mind and flesh. I hope that one day you might allow yourself to reopen that door, with the right trainer. Trust, once broken, is so difficult to mend."

Kynon turned his face away until he'd left.

"Why don't they leave me alone?" he asked later, peevishly, sitting on a stool by the window while Rennick rubbed lotion into his scars. All those visitors, except the one who mattered.

"You're quite the scandal," Rennick said. "For a good three centuries the tribute system has served us well. To be a procurator was to follow a higher path. And now, who knows?"

"But why do you need the tribute system?" Kynon asked. He shook his head. "Oh, I know that it's symbolic and historic and all of that, but why do you bother? You could just as easily have killed us all back in Caralis."

Rennick laughed quietly, massaging the lotion into his shoulders. "But we're better than our ancestors, remember? We don't sacrifice our tributes to the flames." He paused. "Well, we're not supposed to."

Kynon grunted and rolled his eyes.

He told himself he was content living with Rennick in his humble single room. Since his wounds had healed, Rennick had stopped sleeping on the floor. They shared his bed now, and Kynon liked to curl up beside Rennick to sleep. It had never been anything more than companionship. One of the senators had offered him his own apartment on a higher floor, but the idea had terrified Kynon. He hated to think of sleeping alone in the dark. Rennick had seen the panic in his eyes.

"He's all right here with me, Senator," Rennick had told the woman.

It was a true indication of Segasan political values that the woman didn't mind being rebuffed by a lowly captain. "As you wish, Captain, of course."

Rennick was good to him. He had always been good to him, Kynon realized, even back in Caralis. His whipping, five soft strokes, had hardly broken the skin. It had taken Kynon a real whipping to make him realize that. And that was the favor Hera had done him, he supposed.

At night they ate on stools at the little table overlooking the stable yard. Rennick could pick a horse even in the dark.

"There goes Kazer," he would say. "Still a bit lame in the back leg."

"How can you know that's Kazer?" Kynon asked him.

"That's Animon's mare," Rennick said. "I'd know her anywhere. And look, you can just make out the white blaze."

Squinting into the darkness, Kynon could make out very little except a silhouette, but he believed Rennick.

"You know where you are with horses," Rennick said. "You can't just whip a horse to break it in. It's more subtle than that. Treat them right, and they'll be loyal forever. Tomorrow you can come with me, and I'll show you how to look after them. I suppose you always had a stable boy back home?"

Kynon nodded.

The next day he found himself woken at dawn, told to get dressed, and led out to the stables. It was hard work, and Rennick didn't spare him.

"You can handle it," the captain said, and it was all Kynon needed to hear.

He worked all day, stopping only once to eat lunch in the first row of stables, seated on bales of hay listening to the horses stamp and snort. Kynon found the sound comforting. Even the smell of straw and manure was reassuring somehow. He discovered he liked to get his hands dirty. It was good work, hard work, and it distracted him from thinking about the warlord, from dwelling on why he hadn't come.

They washed under the cold stable-yard pump that night and returned to the citadel. It was late, and the dinner the servants had left in Rennick's room was cold. Kynon, too hungry to care, wolfed it down.

He fell asleep as soon as he hit the mattress, lying on his side with his back pressed up against Rennick. If he dreamed, he didn't remember it.

*****

Several days later, Rennick helped Kynon dress again in loose leggings and a flowing shirt. "You have a visitor," he said.

"A visitor?" Kynon asked, his heart skipping a beat. The warlord? No, something in Rennick's voice told him it wasn't. Who, then? He was wary.

He searched Rennick's calm gray-green eyes and was comforted. He trusted Rennick.

"I'll show you," Rennick said.

He led Kynon up through the maze of stairs and passages to a small but opulent reception chamber. He paused at the door. "I will be here. No one will be listening."

Kynon pushed open the door nervously. There was a woman standing with her back to him, gazing out the window into the grand forecourt below them. Kynon's breath caught in his throat as he tried to speak.

"I expected to find you chained at the warlord's feet," she said mildly, turning to face him. She looked older than he remembered. There were circles under her eyes and gray at her temples.

"Mother!" Kynon didn't know whether to laugh or cry. He crossed the floor and embraced her. He tried not to wince as she gripped him tightly.

She pulled back to search his face. "Are you all right?"

Kynon's eyes swam. How could he even begin to explain the last few months to his mother when he didn't understand them himself? He was afraid she would want answers he couldn't give.

"I am better now," he said at last. "There was, there was… It hurt a lot."

The queen's smile was sympathetic. She made a show of inspecting a thread in her sleeve to allow him a moment to compose himself before she spoke.

"And so the warlord invites a representative from Caralis to talk over the finer points of our administration," said the queen. Her clever eyes caught his. "It is a kindness he has not shown to his other conquered territories. I can only assume you have suffered some treatment not shown to his other tributes."

"It wasn't his intention," Kynon said and wondered why the hell he was defending the man.

His mother pursed her lips, evidently wondering the same thing. "Well, your father has sent me to protest to the great senate of Segasa that we simply cannot afford to offer freehold to the serfs."

Kynon raised his eyebrows.

The queen looked at him curiously. "You think it is a wasted effort. So do I." She looked around at the marbled reception hall, which was filled with glorious light. "This is not what I anticipated."

Kynon nodded. "It's quite beautiful."

"It is," his mother agreed. "It is also obscenely wealthy. And the young man who was my escort from the border tells me that it was built entirely with free labor. Can you imagine such a thing?"

Kynon shook his head.

"Neither can I," she replied. "But I am trying my hardest."

"What are you saying?" Kynon asked.

"I'm saying that Segasa is full of surprises." She took his hands in hers and stepped away from him, looking him up and down. "It's good to see you, sweetheart."

The old endearment made his heart swell. He thought he might cry.

"There now," his mother said, raising a hand and brushing his hair back. "It's all right."

What was it about his mother's voice that Kynon almost believed it? It was the same voice that had sung him to sleep as a child, that had told him not to fear thunderstorms and had promised that monsters weren't real. Kynon knew better.

He stepped away from her, breaking their contact, and forced himself to smile. "You're not even going to ask the senate about the freehold, are you?"

"Why should I?" the queen asked. "We both know it's a wasted effort."

"Then what are you going to ask?" Kynon asked. "Now that you are in the enviable position of being owed a kindness by the senate?"

The queen looked at him quietly. "My first thought, Kynon, was to ask for you."

Kynon bit his lip. "You can't do that. Father signed the charter. It would break the peace. And what about the others? Even if the senate allowed it, which they probably wouldn't, I couldn't just leave them here."

His mother smiled at him sadly. "Yes, I know. I quickly came to that realization myself. I just had to know that you had too."

Kynon smiled wryly. His mother had always been sharp. "And the senate?"

"I think," said the queen, drawing a breath, "that I am going to walk in there and ask them how they did it. How they got rid of all their kings and all their gods and became so great."

Kynon's eyes widened, but he didn't doubt she would do it. "What will the king say?"

His mother didn't answer for a long while. She gazed around the room. When she spoke again, she took Kynon by surprise. "I never wanted to marry your father."

Kynon didn't know what to say.

She embraced him again and kissed him gently. "We must make the best of things. I grew to love Jaran very much, despite having been married to him just to further my father's ambitions. Daughters, Kynon, are aware from a young age to expect it. Sons are not."

Kynon saw what she was getting at, and shrugged dismissively. "It doesn't matter. It's over now. He has forgotten about me."

His mother's smile was tinged with sadness. "Try to find a way to be happy here."

"I don't know how," Kynon managed. His eyes filled with tears.

"Find a way," his mother said. Her green eyes refused to let his go. "You must find a way!"

*****

Kynon didn't get to see his mother speak in the senate. He almost wished he had, because the entire citadel was talking about it the next day. Even the servants who passed him in the passageways of the lower part of the citadel were buzzing with interest. The queen from Caralis had put the senators in their place, right there in the senate chamber! She knew sacrifice, and she had dared to demand recompense. A conquered queen, and she was proud and unafraid. She had made the senators and the warlord listen.

Kynon smiled to himself as he heard it told a hundred different ways that day. There was a reason Jaran often sent his queen on diplomatic missions. She had fooled a lot of people in the past. They didn't expect a woman to be so politically astute. And even her husband had underestimated her this time.

His mother had evidently done her research on the journey from Caralis. She knew the history of Segasa. She knew about their gods and their kings and their tributes, and she had dared to turn it all on its head. She was like those ancient Segasans who had told their king they were done with sacrifices and fire and had demanded something new. She had challenged their philosophy in unexpected ways. She hadn't begged. She hadn't pleaded. She had stood before them and said, in words more eloquent than Kynon could imagine, what boiled down to a simple demand: *"Teach me what you know. You owe me that."*

Kynon almost laughed when he thought back to the night he'd played chess with Brasius: *"The queen ought to be used to attack, early and often."*

The queen left Segasa the next evening. She came to see Kynon once more and kissed him and held him and promised she would see him again, and then she left. A depression settled over Kynon when she was gone.

He felt as though her visit should have humiliated him, but he had underestimated his mother. So had the senate. She hadn't dissolved into tears when she saw what Segasa had done to her youngest son. She hadn't thrown herself on the mercy of the senators. She had been fierce and proud.

And she hadn't recoiled from Kynon in private. She hadn't been ashamed at the things that had been done to him and by the things he had done willingly. She loved him still, and Kynon thought that was probably what hurt the most. If she had been disgusted, he wouldn't have missed her so acutely when she was gone.

At night, listening to Rennick snoring on a mattress on the floor, Kynon tried to recall the melodies of the lullabies his mother had once sung to him. He couldn't, and discovered that he was glad. It would be better to forget the person he had been. He wanted to believe that the son, the prince, and the soldier had ceased to exist in any recognizable form. He told himself that only his mother still saw them, but he knew it was a lie. Kynon tried to imagine she had carried them with her when she left, but she hadn't. They were still there. They still poked at his memory, still made their voices heard and reminded him constantly of what had been lost.

He missed his mother.

Tossing and turning that night, ignoring the taut sting in the scars on his bed, Kynon realized something else. He missed Brasius more. The thought hit him with such intense, awful clarity that it took his breath away.

Impossible. It was impossible.

And it was irrational. If he missed anything at all about Brasius, it was purely physical. He missed being touched. He missed the feel of his master's fingers around his cock. He missed the feel of his master plowing roughly into him. He missed the taste of his cum. And most of all, he missed the night where he had lain in his master's bed and explored the warlord's flesh with his trembling fingers. Gods. He'd been breathless with wonder. And when his master had told him to follow his instincts… Kynon groaned, sliding his hand under the blanket to touch his thickening cock before he realized what he was doing.

That was instinct for you. Kynon tried to ignore his erection, rolling over onto his side and bunching the pillow angrily under his head. Gods, what was wrong with him?

He missed fucking. Kynon could allow that.

That was natural, even in the strange forms he had known it since becoming a tribute. But *Brasius*? That made no sense at all. Every kindness the man had ever shown him had been belied by the past few weeks. It was bullshit. All bullshit. If Brasius had ever cared, where the hell was he?

He snorted and rolled over again, thumping the pillow into shape.

Where the hell was he? Kynon's throat swelled with tears. Where the hell was he? Any why the hell couldn't Kynon stay angry? He liked being angry. It made him feel strong. But he could never hold on to it for long when he thought about the warlord. And gods, he thought about the warlord.

The nights were always the worst.

"Tribute," said Rennick in a sleepy tone from beside him. "If you don't shut up, I'll take that pillow and smother you with it."

Kynon snorted again. He knew Rennick was kidding.

******

His mother's visit had changed things. The more he pondered her fierce bravery, the more Kynon began to feel human for the first time in long time. Somehow, he began to reconcile the voices of the son, the prince, and the soldier to himself again. Brasius was wrong. He didn't have to rid himself of them. He *couldn't* rid himself of them. He was a new person, a different person, but he didn't have to be an abomination. He began to speak to the senators and procurators and countless other dignitaries who visited him, in a polite, concise manner. He remembered who he was, and it gave him strength. He conceded nothing. Their own guilt, their own complicity in his torture was theirs to worry about. Kynon discovered he was his mother's son, and he could be proud and fierce in his own way.

"You're a new man," Rennick told him with a smile after one flustered senator had left.

"Hurry up," Kynon told him. "Those horses won't feed themselves."

And later that night, at ease with himself at long last, he felt compelled to talk about it.

"I didn't know what I did wrong," he said as he lay on the bed and Rennick massaged him. "I tried to please them both."

"You didn't do anything wrong," Rennick told him.

"You were always kind to me," said Kynon. He closed his eyes as he felt Rennick trace his hand down the scars on his back. It felt good to be touched, and he trusted Rennick. "I owe you my life."

"You didn't deserve what that bitch did," Rennick said. He slid his hand down to Kynon's buttocks.

Kynon shifted, sighing. He felt peaceful. He wanted this. He wanted to be touched. He wanted to be fucked. It had been too long, and what the hell was he waiting for? For the warlord? Brasius hadn't come. He wasn't going to come. Whatever Kynon had wanted, whatever he had thought they had, it wasn't going to happen. It didn't matter how much he wanted it. That part of his life was over.

And Rennick cared for him. Apart from Alysia, he was probably the only person in Segasa who did. And Kynon didn't want be alone.

"Do you want this?" Rennick asked him.

"You don't just train horses, do you?" Kynon asked him. He felt like they'd been slowly leading up to this moment for days.

Rennick laughed. "If a thoroughbred gets spooked and can't be ridden, they send it my way. You're not my usual patient, I'll admit. Are you offended?"

"No," Kynon said. He liked Rennick too much. "Maybe you should have offered me some oats."

Rennick laughed again and rubbed his buttocks. "Would that have worked?"

"Probably not. I hate porridge," Kynon said and fell silent as Rennick's fingers slipped toward his crease.

"Some of those animals," Rennick said quietly. "They're treated badly once, and they're scared to be touched. They'll shy away from everyone. It takes time with them, and patience. You can't get angry with them for not healing fast enough."

Kynon's heart pounded. "I'm all right. You can keep going."

"No," said Rennick. "I can't."

Kynon twisted his head. "Why not?"

Rennick's gray-green eyes were serious. "It's not my place, tribute."

Kynon tensed. "Whose place is it?"

If he said Brasius, Kynon would punch him. Didn't matter that Rennick was bigger than him, stronger than him; he'd punch him anyway. Brasius hadn't come. He wasn't here. He didn't give a shit.

Rennick pressed his knuckles into Kynon's spine. "You know the answer to that."

Kynon shook his head. "All those important visitors, except one. He can't even face me. So don't you dare tell me I still belong to the warlord!"

Couldn't even say his name aloud.

Rennick didn't say anything. He moved his fingers up to trace Kynon's scars again.

"She gave me those scars so I'd be ugly," Kynon said, trying to keep his voice from breaking. "So he wouldn't want to touch me."

Gods, where had his anger gone? Why couldn't he hold on to it when he thought of Brasius? Was he really that fucking pitiful? Fucking Segasans had got what they wanted after all. They'd broken a prince.

Kynon felt Rennick's breath against his back as he kneaded his muscles. "No. She was threatened by you. For centuries the procurators have been honored by the senate, but without tributes to train, they are nothing. She was afraid the warlord would throw all our traditions out the window because of

LISA HENRY

how he feels about *you*."

Kynon snorted. "How he *feels*? He doesn't feel."

Rennick found a knot in his shoulder and began to work it. "Of course he does. He's not stone. He hates your scars because he feels responsible for them."

"But he isn't," Kynon said, feeling Rennick's fingers skim over the faint bite mark on his shoulder.

"Maybe you ought to tell him that," Rennick said mildly.

Kynon made a face. "Well, where is he?" he demanded. "All this time, where is he?"

"Maybe he's ashamed," Rennick said. "Maybe he's afraid."

"*Afraid!*" Kynon snorted. As if the warlord was ever afraid!

"Maybe he's afraid you'll hate him." Rennick said. "And maybe he won't even admit that to himself, so he spends his days tearing into the senate, throwing his authority around and putting the fear of all our forgotten gods into them."

"You've talked to him?" Kynon felt a jolt of panic.

"Every day," Rennick said in a voice so calm and sure that it didn't feel like a betrayal of their friendship to Kynon. "It was the warlord who sent for your mother, did you know?"

Kynon hid his surprise. He scowled. "To humiliate me, just like with Conal and Arron. His mistake."

"No," said Rennick evenly. "To help you. This time the humiliation was for the senate alone, and she delivered it in spades."

Kynon smiled at that, even as his stomach twisted. To humiliate the *senate*? For what purpose? Not for him. It couldn't be for him, because where was he?

Rennick snorted, amused at the memory. "Their faces! I asked him what he'd done, and you know what he said?"

Kynon shook his head.

Rennick laughed. "He said, 'I played the queen!'"

Kynon's jaw dropped. "Really?"

"Really." Rennick exhaled heavily and grew serious again. "He ripped into the senators like they were nothing. There's nobody else he'd do that for. That was the danger, you see? Hera saw it."

Kynon's muscles tensed. No. There had been nothing between them, not really. Rennick was wrong, and Hera had been wrong, and Kynon had been wrong as well. Because where the hell was he? If there had been something, anything, then why hadn't he come when Kynon needed him?

Kynon swallowed back tears and shook his head. His breath hitched in his throat. "He doesn't even know me."

"He knows enough." Rennick moved his large hands back to Kynon's spine. "You don't remember."

"Remember what?" Kynon asked. He bit his lip.

"It was in Hailon. We were there for some celebration, specially invited because the old duke wanted to show us off as his allies and scare his enemies."

"Hailon," Kynon said, drawing a sharp breath.

"We'd just arrived," Rennick said. "We were heading to our rooms, and suddenly this kid came out of nowhere and smacked straight into Brasius. He should have been shitting himself, but do you know what the cocky little brat said?"

Kynon's throat constricted."'You're in my way.'"

"You do remember," Rennick said, and Kynon heard the smile in his voice.

Kynon drew a shuddering breath. Rennick smelled of sweat and horses. The smell had always comforted him. "I remember."

"Nobody talks to the warlord like that." The smile was still there. "Took me two days to find out your name. And he remembered it, years later, when we came to Caralis."

"For revenge," Kynon said into the mattress. He'd been so sure of it back in Caralis. Now he didn't know what to think.

"No," Rennick said, stroking his hair. "Don't you understand? Because nobody talks to the warlord that way."

Kynon closed his eyes. The bravest, most

stupid thing he'd ever done.

"Nobody talks to the warlord that way," Rennick murmured. "Nobody except you. He remembered that. He tried so hard to get that from you again."

Tears pricked Kynon's eyes, and he didn't know why. They felt something like regret. "It was against the rules."

"Hera's rules," Rennick said, sighing. He shifted away and dropped onto the narrow bed beside Kynon. "And the senate's rules. Never his."

"His tribute, his rules," Kynon said, his voice catching in his throat. *"I want all of you,"* Brasius had said. And all because of that insolent, blustering kid who had refused to show he was scared that day in Hailon. The bravest, most stupid thing he'd ever done. Kynon surprised himself by dropping his head and smiling into the mattress.

Rennick clapped him on the shoulder. "All that time, trying to learn your place. Have you figured it out?"

Kynon caught his breath. He twisted his neck to look at Rennick. "I don't know. Maybe."

"That's my boy," Rennick said with a knowing smile.

Chapter Eleven: Liberation

"Are you sure about this?" Rennick asked, pausing with the razor held an inch above Kynon's chest.

Kynon bit his lip. "Shouldn't I be the one having second thoughts?"

Rennick laughed at that. "Maybe. Hold still, then."

The razor tickled, and Kynon made a face.

It was another sunlit day. Kynon heard the sounds of the horses being exercised in the stable yard outside: thudding hoofbeats, whickering, and the voices of the grooms. Not for the first time he wondered if this was a mistake. A part of him would have preferred to be outside working with the others.

He shook it off. The work in the stables had been good for him, but it wasn't who he was. Prince or tribute, he still wasn't sure himself, but neither of them belonged in the stables. He only knew he was his mother's son and he wouldn't back down. She had faced the senate. He could face the warlord.

Rennick worked slowly, giving Kynon the

chance to relax in the sunlight. It didn't work. Kynon's heart thumped wildly, and he tried to ignore it.

"And you'll come with me?" he asked Rennick.

"As far as I can," Rennick said, wiping down the razor and starting on his abdomen. "As far as you need me."

"Right." Kynon closed his eyes for a moment. "Right."

Rennick began to work the razor carefully around his cock. "One thing you should remember."

"What's that?" Kynon asked.

"You're stronger than you know," Rennick told him. "She didn't break you."

Kynon frowned. "Are you sure about that?"

Rennick straightened up and looked him in the eyes. "Here we are, doing this. How can you even ask that question?"

"I don't feel strong," Kynon admitted.

"I know," Rennick said. "That's why I said you're stronger than you know. Idiot." He wiped Kynon clean with a damp cloth and flicked it against his hip.

"That stings!" Kynon complained.

Rennick raised his eyebrows at Kynon's cock. "Don't pretend you don't like it."

Kynon pushed him away and swung his legs over the edge of the bed. "Thanks, Rennick."

"We're not done yet," Rennick said. The

captain crossed to the table and held up a shirt and jacket. "Try these."

Kynon hadn't worn anything more than loose leggings in weeks, and the clothes felt strange and bulky when he pulled them on, restrictive. A pair of leggings, a light shirt and jacket, and boots, but they might as well have been a suit of armor.

"You look good," Rennick said. "Are you ready?"

Kynon squared his shoulders. "I think so."

He walked through the citadel with Rennick at his side.

"Are you sure I won't see her?" he asked at the bottom of the wide staircase that led to Brasius's apartment.

"She's gone," said Rennick, walking with him up the steps. "I promise. Banished by the senate. Brasius didn't give them much choice about that."

Kynon suppressed a shiver of anxiety as he approached Brasius's apartment, and Rennick gave him a smile of encouragement.

"I'll leave you here," the captain said when they reached the door.

"I don't know what to do," Kynon whispered.

Rennick reached forward and straightened the collar on his jacket. "You'll figure it out. You're strong enough for this."

"Can you come with me?" Kynon asked.

Rennick shook his head. "It's not my place.

Not today." He smiled. "But you ask for me another time, and I'll be here. Go on now." He pushed Kynon gently toward the door.

Kynon lifted his shaking hand to the door. He pushed it open, resisting the urge to look back at Rennick, and then wondered if he should have knocked. It was too late for that now, so he drew a deep breath instead and walked inside.

Brasius was at his desk, working away at something. His handsome face was bathed in light from the window. Kynon studied his face, the angle of his back, the strong hands resting on the desk, and imagined every inch of the lean, muscular body underneath his clothing.

The past few months rushed over Kynon as he stood looking at the warlord. He'd hated the warlord, but it was a strange, fierce sort of hatred that transformed so seamlessly into lust. And underneath the lust there had always been something else. A yearning for approval, a flood of warmth when he won praise, and a desire to please that had nothing to do with physical release. And it felt like they had crossed into something new before Hera had ruined it. Kynon regretted that. Even now his feelings were confused. He needed clarity. He needed answers. It was why he had come here.

"Follow your instincts," Brasius had told him that wondrous night in his bed, and Kynon had trusted his words. Did they still hold true?

Brasius looked up at last, and his eyes widened when he saw Kynon standing there. He stood quickly, almost knocking over his chair. He looked flustered. He cleared his throat.

Nerves? Kynon almost laughed at the thought of it.

"Are you well?" Brasius asked him at last.

"Yes, master," Kynon answered. The reply was automatic, but he was surprised to see Brasius's face darken with a frown. "Have I said something wrong?"

Brasius's mouth tightened. "No."

Kynon felt the sting of panic. Why didn't he like being called *master*? Was it because Brasius no longer considered Kynon his tribute? Kynon thought back to what he'd said to Rennick: *"Don't you dare tell me I still belong to the warlord!"* And Rennick hadn't answered. Gods. That was why. Because Brasius wasn't his master anymore. Brasius didn't want him here at all. He hadn't come to see Kynon in weeks. Why the hell had Kynon let Rennick convince him this was a good idea? Rennick was wrong. Hera had been wrong. And Kynon was wrong as well. Brasius didn't care. Maybe he never had.

Except… Kynon frowned. If that was true, why was Brasius not looking him in the eye? He didn't look much like a warlord now. He looked like something else. Was that doubt shadowing his face? Was it shame? Was it regret? He looked like a man, a normal, human, imperfect man.

Brasius cleared his throat again. He glanced at Kynon quickly and then away again. "Working with Rennick has been good for you. He tells me you are good with the horses."

Kynon frowned. "The horses?"

Brasius leaned back against his desk. His face was unreadable again.

Kynon searched the warlord's face, looking again for the man underneath the monster. Kynon had hoped the warlord might take control. He had always had the knack of getting Kynon to speak aloud the truths he hadn't even realized in himself. But it was apparent Brasius would not encourage him.

"I'm not a stable boy," he said tentatively.

Brasius turned his back for a moment, gathering some pages from his desk. He studied them for a moment. "I'm glad you're well. I hope you prosper in Rennick's care."

Kynon flinched at the note of finality in the warlord's voice. His throat swelled, but he refused to allow the tears to come. No. That wasn't good enough. The warlord had no right to dismiss him like a servant, like a slave. Not after everything. He was owed more than that. He felt like his mother must have, standing in front of the Segasan senate, defeated and defiant at the same time. With nothing else to lose.

Brasius crossed the floor, heading for the bedroom.

Kynon scowled at his back. "I said I'm not a stable boy!"

Brasius turned around, his eyes dark with

anger. "Then tell me what you think you are!"

Kynon drew a deep breath. "I'm your tribute!"

Brasius narrowed his eyes. "Are you?"

"And you are my master," Kynon said, folding his arms across his chest.

He waited for the warlord to refute it, he expected it, but Brasius didn't speak.

Kynon looked past him into the bedroom. Rennick had asked him if he'd figured out his place. And there it was, Kynon knew. Right there, in the warlord's bed. He owed it to himself not to walk away now. Maybe he even owed it to Brasius. He steeled himself for rejection, but he had to know. And right now he had the warlord on his back foot. He pressed his advantage, because he knew it wouldn't last for long.

"Why didn't you come and see me?" he demanded.

Brasius's jaw tightened. "I had a campaign to plan."

Kynon shook his head. "No. That's not good enough."

Brasius raised his eyebrows. "Not good enough?"

"Tell me," Kynon said. He swallowed. "You owe me that much."

Brasius regarded him narrowly for a moment, and Kynon was afraid he wouldn't answer. Nobody spoke to the warlord like that. Just some skinny kid years ago in Hailon Castle. Kynon looked into his face and suddenly knew what he had to do and who he had to be. He had to do the bravest, most stupid thing he'd ever done in his life. Again.

He remembered that dark passageway in Hailon vividly. He remembered how it had felt to have the wind knocked out of him. He remembered the look on the warlord's face: authoritative, annoyed, and *intrigued*.

"Tell me." Kynon moved toward him. Brasius's eyes widened as he approached.

"Go," said Brasius. He shook his head slightly, frowning, and his voice softened. "Walk away."

"I'm not afraid of you." Kynon took a step toward Brasius and looked him in the eye. Then he looked toward the bedroom and back to the warlord. "You're in my way, *master*."

Brasius stared at him for a long moment, and Kynon couldn't breathe. Then the warlord's shoulders relaxed. The frown faded, and his jaw unclenched. His eyes met Kynon's, and astonishingly, his lips twitched. "Am I?"

Kynon nodded, almost dizzy with relief, and sighed as Brasius reached out and ran his fingers down his arm. His flesh prickled. Kynon stepped around the warlord and moved into the bedroom. He crossed to the bed. His heart thumping, he stood beside it. "Tell me why," he said quietly.

Brasius moved slowly into the room. Kynon saw the struggle on his face. "I couldn't," he said at last. His dark eyes shone with something Kynon had never seen there before: uncertainty. "I'm sorry. I was afraid you wouldn't want to see me."

Kynon felt a jolt of surprise. An apology, from the fearsome warlord! No, from the man, Kynon thought. The guilt and the fear. Just a man. He tried to encircle him with his arms, to console him. "It's all right."

Brasius drew away. His face was pale. "I'm sorry."

Gods, he was still apologizing! Kynon wanted to laugh or cry; he didn't know which. But he wanted Brasius more. He'd missed him. He'd missed his touch and his smell. He needed him. Kynon shrugged his jacket off and dropped it to the floor. "Put my collar back on me, master," he said.

Brasius frowned, but his dark eyes gleamed with interest. "Are you sure?"

Kynon nodded. "I need it. I need you."

For a moment he thought Brasius would refuse, but then he moved.

"I wanted this," Brasius said. He retrieved the gold collar from the bureau. "I wanted you to speak your mind."

Kynon trembled at the familiar sensation of the cool gold against his throat, and Brasius reached around him to fasten it. "Feels right."

"You're beautiful," Brasius said. He lowered his head and kissed Kynon's throat softly before looking up to meet his eyes. "I'm so sorry for what happened."

Kynon saw the guilt in the warlord's dark eyes and was almost overcome. He ran his trembling hand along Brasius's shoulder, feeling the muscles underneath the skin. "It wasn't your fault."

And saying it, he realized that he meant it.

Brasius shook his head and frowned. "I should have… She should never…"

"Don't," Kynon said. He ran his hands through his master's hair, drawing him closer. "Not now."

Kynon didn't want Hera to ruin this moment, just like she'd manipulated him into ruining so many others. So many lost opportunities when he'd wanted to speak, wanted to reciprocate, and believed somehow that it was better to be dumb and docile. Believed somehow that that was what was proper. She'd trained fear and doubt into him instead of trust. She had undermined his every instinct. But she was gone now, and she wouldn't ruin it for him again.

Kynon let his head fall back as Brasius mapped the skin of his throat with his lips and teeth. "Wasn't your fault," he murmured.

"I should have seen it, and I should have stopped it," Brasius said. His breath was hot against Kynon's skin. He pressed his lips against the pulse in Kynon's throat.

"Wasn't your fault," Kynon repeated. His heart thumped. "But you should've come."

"Couldn't," Brasius said, his voice straining. He sighed as his fingers discovered the scars on

Kynon's back through his light shirt, and then he drew back. For a moment Kynon thought it was because of the scars, or because Brasius was ashamed he'd shown weakness. Then his master lifted his arms up and pulled his shirt off him, and Kynon felt a rush of heat when he saw the hunger in the warlord's eyes.

"You shaved," he said with a smile, rubbing his hand against Kynon's smooth chest. He slid it down toward Kynon's abdomen, and Kynon pressed into the touch.

"For you," Kynon said.

Then Brasius was on his knees in front of him, fumbling with the ties on the leggings. Kynon felt the cool air against his skin as the leggings fell free. He looked down, dumbfounded, as Brasius leaned in toward his hardening cock.

"Master," Kynon gasped. Shivers ran up his spine as his master's lips closed over the head of his cock. When his master's tongue grazed the slit in his cockhead, Kynon thought he would come then and there. He legs trembled as he reached out to touch his Brasius's hair uncertainly. "Master, what are you doing?"

Brasius leaned back on his heels. "I'm sucking your cock, Kynon. What do you think?"

Kynon snorted with astonishment.

"Shall I continue?" the warlord asked.

"Gods, please, yes," Kynon said, biting his lip.

Kynon closed his eyes, afraid looking at his

master would make him come too soon. His master
swirled his tongue around his cockhead, and Kynon
remembered the first time he'd done this for
Brasius. The strange feel of it, rigid and yielding at
the same time. He'd been so frightened, so
disgusted, but he had learned to love the taste of his
master's cock. He loved to work it, loved to make
the warlord tremble with need. He loved to swallow
his master's cum.

His legs trembled. His spine was liquid.

Brasius took him deeper in his throat, and
Kynon's cock twitched. "Master," he murmured.
His balls tightened.

Brasius groaned, and Kynon felt the
vibrations run up the length of his cock to the base.
Kynon came then, jerking and shaking. He cried out
and looked down in time to see his master
swallowing.

Brasius stood, leaned down to kiss him, and
Kynon tasted his cum in his master's mouth.

"Chain me," Kynon murmured, "fuck me.
Make me yours again."

Brasius growled and pushed him down onto
the bed. Kynon landed on his back, his leggings still
tangled around his ankles. He struggled to kick
them free. Brasius was on top of him immediately,
his mouth tugging at the rings in his nipples. Kynon
arched his back, raising his hands above his head.

"Please, master, chain me!"

Brasius straddled him, reaching up to fasten
his wrists into the retractable cuffs. "Gonna fuck

you hard, tribute."

"Shut up and get on with it!" Kynon retorted, and Brasius laughed.

Brasius moved down between his legs. Kynon gasped and almost leaped off the bed as his master's tongue laved his anus, lubricating him. Kynon raised his knees and spread them, groaning as Brasius pressed a finger into his anus.

"More," he demanded. He squirmed as a second finger joined the first and then a third, and they scissored inside him.

Brasius removed his fingers and hooked Kynon's legs over his shoulders, almost lifting him off the bed. He gripped his cock in one hand and guided it inside Kynon's ass. Kynon writhed and groaned, feeling his master stretch him and claim him for the first time in too long. It felt right.

Brasius pushed in all the way, and Kynon gasped with the effort of taking him all at once. He squeezed his eyes shut, loving the peculiar mix of pain and pleasure. Of total fulfillment.

"Are you all right?" Brasius asked him, breathing hard.

Kynon opened his eyes. "How does it feel, master?"

"Feels so fucking good, boy," Brasius managed.

"Move," Kynon said, holding his master's gaze. "Fuck me, master."

Brasius growled again and began to thrust. He held Kynon's legs over his shoulders, and each heavy thrust caused Kynon to cry out. The angle of penetration caused him to feel every inch of Brasius's cock pounding into his needy flesh. Kynon bit his lip, refusing to close his eyes, loving the strained look on his master's face as Brasius fucked him deeply.

Brasius thrust again and froze suddenly. Kynon squeezed his muscles around his master's spasming cock as Brasius came, and felt himself come as well. He shuddered wildly, crying out while he milked his master's cock for every last drop.

Brasius pulled out and leaned forward. He kissed Kynon deeply, and Kynon wrapped his legs around his master's thighs. His entire body was suffused with pleasure. He sighed.

Brasius licked the side of his face. "Missed you, tribute."

Kynon sighed. His sticky cum lubricated their stomachs as they moved against each another. "Missed you too, master."

Brasius looked down at him. A tender smile played around his lips, lighting up his face and causing tiny crinkles to appear around his eyes. He raised a trembling hand to trace the outline of Kynon's lips. "Love you, tribute."

Kynon didn't hesitate. "Love you too, master."

*****

Later, Kynon felt Brasius move.

"Don't leave me," he murmured. The past

few hours had felt like a dream, and Kynon didn't want to wake yet. He had never felt so comfortable. He had never felt so at peace.

Brasius settled back again, drawing Kynon into his arms. Kynon felt his master's chest against his back, his cock against the crease of his ass, and his strong arms encircling him.

"I will leave you," Brasius said. "Often and for long periods. But I will always come back to you."

Kynon grunted. "And what will I do when you're out conquering the world?"

"That's up to you," Brasius said.

Kynon turned in his embrace, looking at the warlord's face closely in the darkness. "What do you mean it's up to me?"

Brasius tilted his head and kissed him softly on the lips. "I mean your servitude is finished. You must stay here in Segasa, but you will no longer be chained or displayed."

Kynon drew away, reaching up to feel his collar.

"What's the matter?" Brasius asked.

Heat rose in Kynon's cheeks. "I like being chained for you! I thought you liked it too. You liked it an hour ago!"

Brasius laughed. "I did like it. I *do* like it, Kynon. And if you want to be chained here in the privacy of my apartment, I'll always be glad to chain you. But outside of these rooms, you are now your own man."

Kynon was silent.

Brasius reached out to stroke his cheek. "Are you all right?"

"*Mmm.*" Kynon frowned. "I haven't been my own man in so long, I don't remember... Actually, I don't think I've ever been my own man. I was always someone's son, someone's prince, someone's soldier, and someone's tribute."

Brasius drew him closer, running a hand along his hip. "Then today you can begin to know yourself. And I'm going to help you."

Kynon squirmed as Brasius found his nipple rings and twisted them one by one. "I'm keeping those."

Brasius nestled closer to him and flicked one of the rings with his tongue. "I'm glad to hear it."

Kynon ran his fingers through the warlord's hair. "And you'll always come back to me?"

"I promise," Brasius murmured, taking a ring in his teeth and tugging it.

Kynon's cock hardened. "I'll hold you to that."

Brasius shifted and kissed him again. "You won't have to," he said in a low voice. "There is nothing in this world that can stop me from coming back to you. Do you understand that?"

Kynon smiled. "Yes, I understand."

*****

Eight Months Later

Kynon was blindfolded. He tensed as he felt Brasius beside him and leaned toward the warlord's warmth. Brasius's hand on his shoulder guided him.

"Where are we going?" he asked for the third time. "This is supposed to be your homecoming. How can I watch the fireworks if I'm blindfolded?"

"You used to be scared of fireworks," Brasius teased him.

"I like them now," Kynon said, twisting around into Brasius's embrace. He lifted his face and nuzzled against the warlord's throat. He'd missed him. He didn't want to play games. He'd waited four months for the warlord to return to Segasa, worrying each long day away with Alysia. He'd watched the interminable parade through the city from their bedroom window, sat through the lengthy speeches of praise in the senate, and now Brasius was toying with him. He wanted to rip the blindfold off and drag Brasius upstairs to bed.

Brasius laughed as Kynon nipped at his throat with his teeth. "You have missed me, haven't you? And only four months as well! What if they'd been as determined as you Caralians?"

"Let's go upstairs," Kynon said and groaned as Brasius turned him firmly around and began guiding him again. "At least tell me where we're going!"

"I told you, Kynon, it's a surprise," Brasius said.

"I hate surprises," Kynon said.

Brasius stopped, pulling Kynon back by the shirt. He reached down and squeezed his cock. "You *love* surprises."

Kynon ground his hips against him. "Maybe. Where are we going, Brasius?"

Brasius took off the blindfold.

It was a training room, but not like the one he remembered from Hera's instruction. This one was empty and only gave away its purpose because there was a hooded and bound youth kneeling on the tiled floor. He twisted his head wildly as he heard them, but didn't dare move.

"What's this?" Kynon asked curiously. He was no longer scared of the training rooms. Not since Brasius had promised nothing would ever happen in there that Kynon didn't want to happen. Not since Brasius had spent hours with him showing him the finer arts of the training rooms. He had promised Kynon he would know himself, and Kynon loved that Brasius had been the one to teach him.

"It's a tribute," Brasius said. "Untouched. Untrained. Yours, if you want."

"Why the hell would I want a tribute?" Kynon asked. He frowned.

"To master another man, you have to master yourself," Brasius said. He kissed him lightly. "You're ready for this, you're *more* than ready for this, and this isn't just any tribute. Jorell thought you might like this one. Apparently Alysia doesn't want him in their bed."

"And he thought *I* would?" Kynon asked. "I don't want some fresh blood distracting you from me."

He'd been nervous enough inviting Rennick to join them some nights, and he liked and trusted Rennick. He didn't want a stranger, he couldn't trust a stranger, and he'd thought Brasius understood that.

Brasius smiled at his tone. "As if that would ever happen. As if it could!" He grew serious. "But this is all for you. You can bring in whatever equipment you want. You can use whoever you want. You can even refuse if you want."

"Why are you asking me this?" Kynon walked over to the tribute.

"Because I owe you this," Brasius said.

Kynon could see the youth's thigh muscles straining from holding himself in position for so long. Kynon remembered that sensation well — the slow burn. The tribute's hands were chained behind his back. He had a good ass. Kynon moved around in front of him. The tribute sensed his presence and flinched. His cock was half-hard, from the procurators' blend, from fear, and from anticipation. Kynon could hear him breathing heavily from under the cloth hood.

"You *owe* me?" Kynon asked Brasius, raising his eyebrows. "What could you possibly owe me? You've given me everything."

"This is a special tribute, my love," Brasius

said. He moved behind Kynon, clasped him tightly, and slipped one hand down the loose collar of his shirt to toy with the rings in his nipples. "Straight from Lutrica."

"A special tribute?" Kynon asked. His cock began to stiffen as Brasius played with his ringed nipples, pinching and squeezing them.

"Have a look." Brasius's voice was low.

His hand trembling, Kynon reached forward and slowly drew off the hood.

Frightened blue eyes stared back at him from a face framed in golden hair.

Kynon leaned back against Brasius as the warlord's other hand slipped down the front of his leggings to find his cock. He smiled at the trembling tribute. "Hello, Conal. Welcome to Segasa."

"Kynon!" Conal's voice was ragged. Tears brimmed in his wide blue eyes and slipped down his flushed face. "Gods, Kynon! Please!"

"Didn't the procurators tell you not to speak unless it's to answer a question?" Kynon asked him quietly.

Conal stared up at him, choking back a sob.

Brasius released Kynon, turning him around. He looked at him questioningly.

Kynon smiled at the uncertainty in the warlord's face. "He's my friend," he said. "Whatever happened, he will always be my friend. And he can find his place here as well, can't he?"

Brasius smiled, leaning forward to kiss Kynon. "If you can show him how."

Kynon glanced down at Conal. "I can," he said soundly. "I will. And it doesn't have to hurt, does it? There's another way."

"There's another way," Brasius agreed with a smile.

Conal gazed back fearfully.

Brasius kissed him again, and Kynon closed his eyes. He slipped his arms around Brasius, opening his lips to the gentle pressure of Brasius's tongue. He'd missed him so much, but those four long months of worry and frustration drained away as they kissed. Brasius was holding him tightly, there was nowhere in the world he would rather be, and tonight there would be fireworks.

ABOUT THE AUTHOR

LISA HENRY likes to tell stories, mostly with hot guys and happily ever afters.

Lisa lives in tropical North Queensland, Australia. She doesn't know why, because she hates the heat, but she suspects she's too lazy to move. She spends half her time slaving away as a government minion, and the other half plotting her escape.

She attended university at sixteen, not because she was a child prodigy or anything, but because of a mix-up between international school systems early in life. She studied history and English, neither of them very thoroughly.

She shares her house with too many cats, a green tree frog that swims in the toilet, and as many possums as can break in every night. This is not how she imagined life as a grown-up.

ALSO BY LISA HENRY

The California Dashwoods
Two Man Station
Adulting 101
Sweetwater
He Is Worthy
The Island
One Perfect Night
Fallout, with M. Caspian
Dark Space
Darker Space (Dark Space #2)

Playing the Fool series, with J.A. Rock
The Two Gentlemen of Altona
The Merchant of Death
Tempest

With J.A. Rock

The Preacher's Son
When All the World Sleeps
Another Man's Treasure
Mark Cooper versus America (Prescott College #1)
Brandon Mills versus the V-Card (Prescott College #2)
The Good Boy (The Boy #1)
The Naughty Boy (The Boy #1.5)
The Boy Who Belonged (The Boy #2)
Fall on Your Knees

Made in the USA
San Bernardino, CA
13 July 2020